"I suppose you consider yourself some sort of expert on kissing?"

The glint in his eyes spelled danger. "Is that a challenge…?"

She pressed a hand to her throat; she could feel the vibration of her pulse through her fingertips. "Most definitely n-not." Her attempt to sound firm and faintly amused by his response failed abysmally. "I'm quite willing to accept you are the world's best kisser without a demonstration." Her laughter faded away in the face of his unblinking expressionless stare. "You didn't come here to kiss me," she protested.

A strange expression flickered in his dark eyes. "Didn't I?" He gave a twisted smile that changed into a look of deadly intent. "Then if I didn't, I should have…"

Kim Lawrence

THE SPANIARD'S LOVE-CHILD

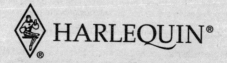

TORONTO • NEW YORK • LONDON
AMSTERDAM • PARIS • SYDNEY • HAMBURG
STOCKHOLM • ATHENS • TOKYO • MILAN • MADRID
PRAGUE • WARSAW • BUDAPEST • AUCKLAND

ISBN 0-373-12456-2

THE SPANIARD'S LOVE-CHILD

First North American Publication 2005.

This edition published by arrangement with Harlequin Books S.A.

® and TM are trademarks of the publisher. Trademarks indicated with
® are registered in the United States Patent and Trademark Office, the
Canadian Trade Marks Office and in other countries.

www.eHarlequin.com

Printed in U.S.A.

CHAPTER ONE

'MOTHER, you must rest.' Raul Carreras gently pushed his mother back onto the pile of pillows, his eyes anxiously scanning her pale face.

She looked close to collapse, which was hardly surprising: ill health, losing a husband and son so recently had already taken its toll. He feared this was one blow too many.

'I do not want to rest, Raul!' Aria Carreras cried fretfully, pushing aside the blanket he had pulled across her legs. 'Do not treat me like a child. My grandchildren have been kidnapped. They are God knows where. Perhaps not even alive...' Her voice rose to a shrill crescendo before her eyes filled with tears.

As he watched her press her shaking hand to her mouth to stifle the whimper of distress that emerged from her trembling lips the skin drawn across Raul's chiselled features tautened. Right now he might have to accept that he was helpless to ease her pain, but one day, he vowed silently, someone would pay!

Aria Carreras succeeded in fighting back the tears. 'And you ask me to *rest*...?'

'Firstly, we don't know for certain that the children have been kidnapped...'

'But you think they have been?' his mother accused shrilly. 'If only your father was here he would know what to do. If he'd been here it wouldn't have happened. *He* wouldn't have let it.'

She looked up and caught the spasm of pain momentarily

5

disturb the composure of her son's face. An expression of contrition spread across her own fine-boned features; Raul so rarely allowed those around him to see his feelings that everyone, including to her shame herself, tended to overlook the fact he had any.

She reached up and took her son's hand.

'I'm sorry, that was unfair. You have improved our security beyond recognition.'

Raul returned the pressure of her fingers and smiled, but kept to himself the grim reflection that his improved security had not stopped people entering their home and taking away two children without anyone raising the alarm.

So much for modern technology!

'And if your father had been alive by now he would have shouted at everyone, alienated the police and caused a diplomatic incident.'

'At the very least,' Raul agreed with the faintest glimmer of a smile in his dark eyes. His expression grew grave as he sat down on the edge of the bed. 'Now what you must do is trust me to do what should be done. I *will* get Katerina and Antonio back, you know that?'

If anyone else had made that claim she would have automatically considered it an attempt to assuage her anxieties, but Raul was one of those rare individuals who never promised anything he couldn't deliver. Aria lifted her hand to her son's lean face. There was an expression on his dark features that she was not familiar with; his business rivals would have been.

'I know that,' she agreed, despite everything relaxing slightly.

'Then will you take the sedation the doctor has prescribed?'

Aria sighed and gave a rueful smile. 'If I must.'

Her son kissed her on both cheeks and promised that he

would speak to her as soon as he knew more. On the way out he had a quiet word with the maid who had been hovering discreetly in the background and then, with a last smile for his mother, he left the room.

The senior detective who had been assigned to the case turned from his female colleague as the tall figure of Raul Carreras quietly re-entered the room. Unlike the other members of the besieged household, the head of the family was not wearing night clothes, but a dark well-cut business suit and shirt; the loosening of the knot of his silk tie was the only concession he had made to the hour and the circumstances.

'How is Mrs Carreras?' the detective enquired solicitously.

'The doctor has sedated my mother.'

Their eyes clashed and the comforting hand the detective had been about to place on the younger man's shoulder was hastily thrust back into his pocket. He waited silently as the tall dark-haired figure shrugged off his jacket and draped it around the back of a gilded Louis XIV chair, feeling a flicker of nostalgia tinged with envy as his observant eyes noted the suggestion of tight, well-developed muscles shift underneath the fine fabric.

Chief Superintendent Pritchard had dealt with a number of kidnapping cases during his career and he was accustomed to seeing the families involved fall apart. He knew all the right things to say in such circumstances, but it was clear this was not an instance where sympathy was either required or desired.

Not everyone reacted the same way, of course, he privately conceded, though nobody he'd come across had displayed quite so much monumental control as this man. It was impossible to tell from his demeanour what Raul Carreras was feeling—or if he was feeling anything at all.

Maybe the guy would fall apart at some point but, he thought, flicking a covert glance at the strong profile of a man who had enough clout to make the Commissioner ring him personally to remind him how important this case was, he rather doubted it.

'So where do we go from here?' Raul asked.

'There are set procedures, sir.'

For the first time some of Raul's frustration threatened to slip past the careful guard he had erected. Impotence building inside him made him feel as though he were in danger of imploding, or at the very least smashing something. But, he reminded himself, the things, the *people*, he wanted to smash were not here. Taking a deep breath, he forced his hands, clenched into tight, white-knuckled fists, to loosen.

Focus!

Losing it was an indulgence he couldn't afford, and as for thinking about what might be happening to the children, he knew he couldn't go there. He couldn't afford to give into the gut-wrenching fear or his anger. He needed to stay in control not just of the situation, but of himself.

'You are the professional, and I will listen to your advice...'

The detective's expression remained wary as the sculpted lips lifted fractionally at the corners, forming a cold smile that did not touch the tall Spaniard's eyes.

'So long as I consider what you suggest is in the best interests of getting my nephew and niece back safely,' he qualified simply.

'It was you who discovered they were missing, is that right?'

A slight inclination of Raul's dark head confirmed this.

'It is my habit to look in on them before I retire for the night.' Raul swallowed convulsively and his eyes darkened.

The detective was sympathetic. 'A shock?'

'Yes.' Raul's dark lashes came down like a shield. 'How many of them were there, Superintendent? What does the security footage show?'

The permanent indentation above Raul's aquiline nose deepened as he observed the air of forced optimism on the older man's face falter. One dark-winged brow rose.

'There is a problem?' he queried harshly.

The older man struggled to maintain eye contact—pretty crazy when you considered all the hard men he had faced down over the years—and nodded. 'There's nothing on the security tapes, I'm afraid.'

At the policeman's rueful admission a muscle clenched in Raul's lean cheek. *'Nothing?'*

A nod.

'Por Dios!' The breath whistled silently from Raul's lungs through his clenched teeth.

'In cases like this we have to consider the possibility of an insider involvement.'

'I imagine you must. You may question the staff, but they have my total confidence,' Raul stated firmly. 'All are loyal to our family.'

The detective, who was too diplomatic to say he found such trust naïve in this day and age, changed the subject. 'Your security system is computerised...'

'Isn't everything?'

'I'm afraid it's been tampered with.'

'This system is meant to be foolproof,' Raul spat out.

'In my experience there is no such thing, sir,' came the blunt reply to this harsh observation. 'I'm afraid this wasn't any opportunist crime; these people aren't amateurs,' he admitted with a sigh. 'We're dealing with people who knew exactly what they were doing.'

There were thirty seconds of complete silence during which the police officer found himself subjected once more to the penetrating scrutiny of silver-shot midnight eyes.

'And do you know what *you're* doing, Superintendent?'

Clearly if he gave the wrong answer to this deceptively soft question he could say goodbye to co-operation, and the last thing he needed at this stage was the tycoon importing some sort of private army. 'Well, I'm...'

A hand was held up. 'Modesty does not interest me,' Raul explained tersely. 'Competence does.'

'I'm good at what I do.'

Raul nodded. 'Fine, then what happens next?'

'We wait to hear from the kidnappers. We have traces on the line, of course, but...' He shrugged.

'These people know what they are doing,' Raul inserted.

'People make mistakes, Mr Carreras.' The officer cleared his throat. 'I take it you will have no problem...financially speaking, of responding to any ransom demand?'

'I will do whatever it takes—within the law, naturally.'

The ironic little rider worried the seasoned detective. 'I just have to check. Mr Carreras, you really mustn't lose hope or do anything rash.' A good judge of character, Alan had decided within seconds of being introduced to this man that Raul Carreras was quite capable of taking the law into his own hands. 'There's a really excellent chance at this stage of us getting the children back unharmed.'

'And the people responsible for their abduction suitably punished.'

The policeman looked away from those hard eyes and astonishingly felt a flicker of pity for the perpetrators. Oh, my God, did they pick on the wrong guy to mess with. Without a word being said he knew that Raul Carreras would hunt down the men or women who had harmed members of his family—even if it took him the rest of his life.

Antonio had been easy; the exhausted little boy had tumbled into her own still-warm bed and fallen asleep almost immediately. It had taken Nell a good hour to calm Katerina to a degree where she could pick up the phone without the hysterical teenager calling her a traitor and threatening to run away—*again*!

Nell, afraid that she would carry out her threat, had listened as the young girl unburdened herself. Not far into the emotional tirade it became clear to Nell that, even allowing for exaggeration on Katerina's part, Raul Carreras, the uncle who had become the children's guardian since their father's death the previous month, had handled the entire matter with the sensitivity of a ten-ton truck.

God, what an idiot the man is, she thought scornfully as Katerina described an incident that had occurred the previous weekend. To turn up at a party and drag her back home in front of all her friends had been bad enough, but Raul Carreras, it transpired, had made things infinitely worse by first telling his niece to wash the paint off her face because she looked ridiculous!

His autocratic and insensitive behaviour, Nell reflected, might have been deliberately calculated to evoke rebellion in a teenager who had been used to a much more relaxed form of discipline.

All the while Nell had listened to Katerina's list of grievances she had been increasingly aware of the anxiety their disappearance must be causing back at the Carreras household; it didn't seem likely that they wouldn't have been missed by now. In fact, considering the sort of intrusive security that Katerina was complaining about, it seemed incredible that the children could simply have walked out of the house.

'If there are so many cameras everywhere surely someone must have noticed you leaving?'

'I fixed them,' Katerina explained with a contemptuous little shrug. 'It was kid's stuff,' she elaborated.

A computer illiterate Nell tried not to look intimidated by this casual disclosure.

'Don't worry, the system was only down long enough for us to get out, the family silver will be safe.'

'I'm sure they care more about you than the family silver.'

'You think?' the teenager drawled cynically.

'They're probably worried sick.'

'I don't care!'

'I don't believe that, Kate,' Nell inserted gently.

'All right, but they're *not* my family!' Katerina snarled defiantly before scribbling down a number on the jotter beside the phone and handing it to Nell and adding angrily, 'You're more my family than they are. They never had any time for Dad because he wouldn't marry who they wanted. Not once, not even when Mum was ill, did they contact him.'

'Well, there's no good being bitter about it, Kate, because your dad wasn't, was he?'

Katerina responded to Nell's gentle challenge with a watery grin. 'Dad was never mad with anyone for very long.'

And especially his daughter, whom he had indulged outrageously, Nell reflected, passing the tearful girl a tissue. A girl less sweet-natured and sensible than Katerina might have been spoilt by such indulgent parenting, Nell thought fondly as she enfolded the girl in a quick hug.

'And he wouldn't want you to be either.' Both sets of

eyes, one brown and one cornflower-blue, held tears as they drew apart.

'Your uncle Raul was pretty young when your dad fought with his family, so he can't have been involved with what went on back then…' Nell reasoned, firmly ignoring her own personal and possibly irrational prejudices on the subject. 'Maybe you should give him a chance?' she suggested tentatively. 'This is a learning experience for you all.'

'*Maybe*…but maybe *he* shouldn't try to make me learn Spanish.'

The childish complaint made Nell burst out laughing. 'That doesn't seem unreasonable, Kate, considering you are half Spanish and you know your dad always regretted not having brought you up bilingually.'

'Well, what about sending Antonio to some posh boarding-school? Do you think that's reasonable?' Katerina gave a tiny crow of triumph as she saw the expression of disapproval chase across the older girl's fair-skinned and expressive features. Her soft mouth firmed. 'Antonio needs me!' Abruptly her pretty face crumpled. 'When you call, tell them we're not coming back!' On this throbbing note she ran into the bathroom and locked the door behind her.

Feeling totally helpless as she listened to the noisy sound of sobbing, Nell sadly dialled the number Katerina had given her. If there was anything in her power she could do to make this easier for Javier's children, she would, she resolved, squaring her slender shoulders.

'Hello, I'm sorry to disturb you at this hour, but would it be possible for me to speak to Mrs Carreras?' Nell decided at the last second that Katerina's case might find a more sympathetic ear with her grandmother than her uncle—*and it's got nothing whatever to do with the fact just thinking about the man spooks you?*

Katerina, who had emerged from the bathroom, took up a cross-legged posture on the sofa. 'It's no good, she'll do whatever *he* says. Everyone does!'

At this resentful observation an image of a dark fallen angel face rose up before Nell's eyes and she recalled the last and only time she had seen Raul Carreras.

He had made quite an impression! But then Raul Carreras wasn't the sort of man you forgot in a hurry. A shiver traced a shaky pathway down her spine as she recalled the extent to which the clinical touch of those hooded midnight eyes had disturbed her.

The family had been swept away from the funeral in a fleet of shiny black limos and the last of Javier's own colourful art-world friends had drifted away, but one figure had remained. The image of the tall, broad-shouldered, black-clad figure, head bowed slightly against the first flurries of snow, standing alone beside the grave had indelibly imprinted in Nell's brain, as were the words they had exchanged afterwards.

She had thought her own presence amongst the trees at the edge of the cemetery had gone unnoticed until he had lifted his head and looked directly at her.

Nell had immediately been able to see the resemblance between the Carreras brothers, both golden-skinned, and black-haired; facially too there were similarities, though these were not strong. Javier's warm smile and natural exuberance for life had made people overlook the fact his features were neither symmetrical nor in proportion, but his brother possessed bone structure that was *achingly* perfect.

Though it had been the combination of a broad, intelligent forehead, strong, chiselled cheekbones, wide, mobile mouth and incredible thickly lashed dark eyes that had made her stare at Raul Carreras, it had been something else that had made her incapable of stopping!

Raul Carreras was quite simply the sexiest man she had ever seen. Furthermore what he projected didn't come across as in any way cultivated or contrived, it was simply an intrinsic part of the man and, unlike the clothes he wore, it was unrefined and raw.

After a few seconds one dark, strongly defined brow had lifted.

Aware that her mouth was unattractively open, Nell had closed it hastily and stepped forward, feeling irrationally like an intruder. 'I'm sorry, I didn't mean to startle you.' Beneath her feet the frosted grass crunched.

He looked at her with cold eyes that held a deeply ingrained cynicism. 'I am not startled,' the unsmiling figure retorted sardonically.

'I'm—'

'I know who you are.'

The inexplicable hostility shining in those impenetrable, lustrously lashed eyes had brought a look of uncertainty to her face. 'How are the children?'

All Nell's attempts to see or at least speak to them in the days following Javier's death had been obstructed by staff at the Carreras household. They had politely listened to her explain that she was a friend of the family and then repeated that no member of the family was at that time available, but her condolences would be passed on.

She had briefly considered presenting herself at the house and explaining things in person, but on reflection had dropped the idea. The family had enough to deal with; she would see the children at the funeral and sort things out then.

'As you would expect them to be considering they've just lost their father.'

Nell's soft mouth twisted in an apologetic grimace. 'It was a stupid question.'

'Yes.'

Nell blinked. There was blunt and then again there was damned right deliberately rude. She had no doubt whatever into which category his response fell. Once more his antagonism puzzled her.

'Would it be an intrusion if I came to the house?'

'Yes.'

Thinking he had misunderstood what she had said, Nell repeated herself.

Raul Carreras took a step towards her and Nell's mouth went dry. He was a great deal taller than most Spaniards she had met—several inches over six feet, she judged. And whereas Javier had been a compact, slightly built man, his brother, though lean, possessed broad shoulders and the long legs of a natural athlete.

'Friends and family only are invited back to the house.' *And you are neither.* Though the words were not said it was obvious that was what he meant. As put-downs went this was masterful.

A shocked and hurt Nell was left staring after his retreating back.

CHAPTER TWO

WITH difficulty Nell dragged her thoughts back from the cold place they had taken her to. She covered the receiver with her hand and sent Katerina a pained look of appeal.

'Hush,' she pleaded. 'It's a terrible line. I won't be able to hear what they're saying, Kate.'

'I'm afraid Mrs Carreras is not available. Would you like to speak to Mr Carreras?'

Since when were Spanish billionaires so damned conveniently accessible? Just my luck! Nell sighed and applied herself to the unenviable task in hand.

'I suppose I'll have to.' A frown furrowed her smooth brow as it occurred to her that they hadn't even asked her to identify herself.

'This is Raul Carreras.'

The voice, deep and slightly accented, was just as she recalled. She rubbed her bare forearms where a rash of goose-bumps had unaccountably broken out.

'Mr Carreras, you probably don't remember who I am… The thing is, you might not have noticed yet, but the children, Antonio and Katerina…' She closed her eyes—*as if he doesn't know their names!* She took a deep breath. 'They're not there, but,' she added hastily, 'I have them and they're perfectly safe.'

'Perhaps I should speak to them to confirm that for myself…?'

Nell, who had been expecting a lot of hows and whys, was actually quite relieved by what seemed like a pretty moderate response under the circumstances. She held the phone out to Katerina and pointed at the receiver mouthing, Speak to him. The girl, with a mulish expression, shook her pretty head negatively in response and folded her arms across her chest.

'I'm sorry, Mr Carreras, but now might not be a good time.'

'And when might be a good time?'

Even the other side of the city the voice had enough chill in it to freeze flesh. Perhaps Katerina hadn't exaggerated about her uncle's callous temperament? Perhaps his behaviour was prompted not by ignorance of how to respond to the needs of the orphaned children, but a genuine cold and unfeeling nature.

'Well, that depends…'

'I'm never going to see him—*never*!' Katerina declared dramatically.

'Katerina, I thought we decided you were going to be sensible. I'm sorry about that,' she added down the phone where for several seconds she could only hear the sound of heavy breathing. 'Are you still there?'

'I'm still here. What do you want me to do?'

The abrupt question surprised Nell. Raul Carreras was the last man in the world she could imagine asking for advice. Perhaps she had done the man an injustice? she mused.

Perhaps he was finding the adjustment just as hard to make as the children were? It couldn't be easy finding yourself landed with two children you barely knew.

'Tell me what you want and it is yours.'

'What I want?' she echoed, bewildered by the harsh statement. 'It's not a question of what I want.'

'Then let me talk to the person who decides such matters.'

Nell took the harsh request to be ironic—the sort of request for divine intervention that a man who didn't know what to do might make.

'You have to appreciate, Mr Carreras, the children feel very vulnerable at the moment,' she began tentatively. 'They've had such a lot of upheaval and changes in their lives.' *God, talk about platitudes!* 'Their father's death was so awfully sudden and…listen,' she added in a rush, 'I don't want to tell you how to bring up the children.' *Though maybe someone should because you're making a hell of a mess of it.* 'But maybe if you sat down and discussed things with them?'

'I thought I wasn't permitted to talk to the children.'

'I know this must be frustrating,' she replied sympathetically. 'But you have to be patient.'

'You are stretching my patience.'

'Oh, for goodness' sake!' she shouted, her own frayed patience snapping. 'Can't you stop thinking about yourself for one moment and imagine how the children are feeling right now, Mr Carreras?' You could only carry on giving someone the benefit of the doubt for just so long. 'Other people do.' People like Javier.

'Please be calm.'

'I am calm!' she yelled, and frowned repressively at Katerina who giggled as she made this heated claim.

'I can be very generous.'

Nell gave a sigh of exasperation; did he think he just had to throw money at any problem and it went away?

'This isn't about money,' she reminded him severely.

'Then what is it about—*revenge*?'

'For heaven's sake, don't be so silly.'

Katerina, who was listening carefully to the one-sided conversation, gave a smug smile. 'I told you he's impossible and he won't listen to anything you say. He thinks women are there to look decorative and have babies.'

Nell shot Katerina a warning look and the girl lapsed into sulky silence as Nell attempted to moderate her own tone, regretting deeply that she'd allowed her tongue to run away with her.

'Javier was a pretty laid-back sort of dad...' Her own voice thickened as she thought of Javier with his laughing eyes and wicked sense of humour.

It might be a year since she'd reluctantly moved out of the sprawling, slightly shabby Edwardian villa in the un-fashionable seaside town she had shared with Javier for almost two years, but he had still been very much a part of her life.

She sometimes wondered where she would be now had she not seen Javier in the crowded supermarket that after-noon with two fretful children. She had recognised him immediately, even though she had never attended one of his classes—the famous artist who had occasionally done a guest lecture at the art college she'd attended had been quite a celebrity. She had heard about his young wife's tragic death, of course; the art community had been buzzing with it.

Javier had been charmingly grateful when she had coaxed Antonio out of his hysterics, and if she hadn't taken matters into her own hands that would have been it. But Nell had come up with a brilliant idea, and, driven to take drastic action, she had turned up on Javier's doorstep the next day and suggested an arrangement that would be a solution to both their problems.

'I'm about two steps away from homeless and you need someone to help with your children. For bed and board I'll be that someone.'

Javier hadn't taken her seriously but Nell had persisted and eventually he had agreed to a month's trial. The ar-

rangement had turned out better than either of them had
expected.

'I have no desire to discuss my family with you.' Directly following this frigid, sneering response Nell heard
the sound of a muffled speech in the background as though
someone else was in the room. A woman, maybe? Was he
speaking to her from his bed? Her wayward imagination
threw in a deeply distracting image of a pale-limbed beauty
trailing her teasing fingers down a lean brown muscle-
packed torso.

Her tummy muscles quivered uncomfortably.

'If you are indeed concerned about the children—surely
you must see that the best place for them is with their
family.'

'A family they don't know. Listen, Mr Carreras, the children simply aren't used to the heavy-handed approach.' She
caught her lower lip between her teeth; it was so frustrating
that everything she said came out wrong. 'Not that I'm
saying you're heavy-handed *as such*,' she added hastily.
'But a little bit of give and take…'

'Just who am I speaking to?' It wasn't so much a matter
of something new being in his voice as he made this abrupt
demand, but more an absence of something that up to this
point had been there. With a confused frown Nell identified
this missing factor as restraint and realised that up to this
point the children's uncle had been choosing his words with
care.

'This is Nell Rose; I was a friend of your brother's and
for—'

'*Nell Rose? Por Dios!* I know who you are, Miss Rose.'
The palpable sneer in his cutting voice brought an angry
flush to her pale cheeks. 'Now am I to infer that Antonio
and Katerina are with you, and they came willingly?'

'*Came willingly?*' Nell gave an uncomprehending shake

of her head, then realised he couldn't see her. 'Well, they turned up on my doorstep about an hour and a half ago, so I suppose you could say that.'

She shook her head and ignored Katerina's suspicious hissed, 'what's he saying?'

'And where is *there*?'

Nell gave her address.

'Hold the line,' he demanded abruptly.

'I'm sorry, Superintendent, but it seems as if we are dealing with a runaway not a kidnapping situation,' Raul told the detective who had been listening to the conversation.

'You know this Miss Rose? Is she genuine?'

Raul nodded. Human nature being what it was, the profound relief he had experienced when he had realised that the children had not been snatched had been replaced by a hostility for the woman to whom they had run. A woman who incredibly had had the audacity to instruct him on the finer points of raising children.

'Genuine? Extremely doubtful. She was my brother's mistress. I do not know her personally.'

'She was your brother's partner, but it didn't occur to you that the children might have gone to her?'

Raul, who considered this a fair question, accepted the mild underlying note of criticism in the other man's voice with an expressive shrug.

'They were not together when Javier died; she is not the staying kind.'

Hearing the contemptuous bite in Raul's voice, it occurred to the detective that, for someone who claimed not to be acquainted with the woman in question, Raul Carreras appeared to have formed a very definite opinion of the woman's character.

*   *   *

The time stretched and so did Nell's patience—to breaking-point.

'Miss Rose, are you still there?'

The yawn Nell had been trying to stifle escaped.

'I'm sorry if I'm keeping you awake, but I was just convincing the police that we are not dealing with a kidnapper.'

Nell's jaw snapped shut. *'Kidnapper?'* she yelped. *'Me?'* she added in a weak whisper. 'You're joking, *right*?'

'Wrong, I am not joking.'

'But why on earth would you assume the children had been kidnapped?'

'What would you have assumed, Miss Rose, if you had looked in on them at two in the morning and found them gone from their beds with no explanation?'

At the other end of the phone Nell could not see Raul's eyes darken as he relived the moment he had discovered the children were missing. When, suspicions roused by the inanimate lump in Antonio's bed, he had pulled the covers back and found pillows artistically arranged beneath the quilt, he'd sprung into action. A rapid search of Katerina's room had revealed a second empty bed and he had ordered a search of the house.

While he'd been doing things he had been able to keep the sick feelings of dread at bay. It had been later, after the police had arrived and taken control, that he had been unable to repress his fear.

'You?' Nell couldn't keep the incredulity from her voice. A man who checked in on the sleeping youngsters before he retired for the night did not mesh with Katerina's description of someone who looked on his brother's children as an imposition.

'What?' The irascible voice sounded impatient.

'Well, yes, but *kidnap*, isn't that a little extreme?' she asked faintly.

'What world are you living in? We have a great deal of money and it is a fact of life that there are many people out there—unscrupulous people—who would do anything, and I mean *anything*, to dispossess us of some of it.'

Nell, aware of Katerina's scrutiny, tried not to let her horror at this chilling information show. She couldn't even imagine the sort of life he was describing.

'What are the police going to do now?'

'Police?' Katerina parroted sharply. 'Has he sent the police after us?'

Frowning, Nell shook her head for the girl's benefit and laid a finger to her lips.

'Don't worry, Miss Rose, they are not going to prosecute you for wasting police time.'

Even though Katerina was listening, Nell could not permit this blatant attempt to intimidate her pass. 'Well, they'd have a hard time doing that, wouldn't they?'

'If you'd contacted me as soon as they got there like any normal, responsible adult—if you'd stopped to consider the anguish their family would be feeling instead of waiting for hours—a great deal of grief, not to mention wasting police resources, might have been avoided.'

Nell bit her lip; it was only Katerina's presence that stopped her responding to this unfair accusation with a few home truths of her own. Raul Carreras was in no position to play the blame game.

'Possibly this conversation might be better continued in the morning when everyone has had a little sleep,' she suggested stiffly.

'*Morning!*' A caustic laugh reverberated down the line. 'You think I will permit the children to spend the night under your roof? Tell them I will be there in twenty minutes.'

'My God, you really are as stupid as you look.'

There was the angry hiss of indrawn breath before a cold voice inserted with icy precision. *'Twenty minutes.'*

A martial light entered Nell's blue eyes as she replaced the dead receiver.

'Is he coming? I won't go with him.'

Nell's cool voice cut through the rising note of hysteria in the teenager's voice. 'You look tired, Kate. Why don't you crawl into bed until your uncle gets here?'

'You mean he's going to take us away.'

Over my dead body. 'Nobody's doing anything until the morning,' Nell told the girl calmly.

CHAPTER THREE

THE door opened before Raul had a chance to ring the bell. He sensed she had been waiting for him, watching through the window perhaps, for his car to draw up? He spared a passing thought for his car parked at that moment in a less than salubrious area, and turned his attention to the young woman standing in the doorway.

A woman who looked like this and was prepared to exploit it, as Nell Rose had already proved herself willing and able to do, did not need to live in such a place. There would be men—men like his brother—more than happy to house her in relative luxury, though she would have to make a little more effort with her appearance, he thought, studying her critically. Because whatever else Nell Rose had been doing while she'd waited for him, it had not involved a comb! Her red-gold hair stood like a fiery nimbus around a porcelain-pale face.

The women he became involved with did not have tangled hair; they were well groomed, attractive, intelligent and no more interested in long-term commitment than he was.

It was conceivable their hair might be messy in the morning, but it was not Raul's habit to spend the entire night with a woman. He rose early, and the idea of small talk over breakfast did not appeal to him.

As if sensing his silent condemnation the diminutive redhead lifted her hand to push back the mesh of red-gold waves from a heart-shaped face. Raul, his attention mo-

mentarily diverted, was struck by the extreme slenderness
of her small-boned wrist.

Her hands, like her bare feet, were narrow and small,
and, wearing those slightly ridiculous oversized pyjamas
emblazoned with teddy bears, she didn't actually look very
much older or sophisticated than his rebellious niece. The
woman seemed to possess chameleon-like qualities, but
Raul knew Nell Rose could look very different.

His mind drifted back to the day he had seen her on the
beach with his brother. Her sleek, rounded curves had been
revealed in a bikini of petite and provocative proportions.
He had watched as she had stretched with lazy feline grace
in the sun before rolling over to whisper something in his
brother's ear.

Javier's reply had made her set off down the beach with
him in hot pursuit. He had caught up with her at the water's
edge. Raul had been able to hear her laughs and screams
as Javier had picked her up, from where he had been standing in the sand dunes. When Javier had strode into the sea
until they'd both been immersed by the waves, he had
turned and walked swiftly away.

It had been painful for him to see the brother he'd ad-
mired and respected making a fool of himself over a girl
who'd been so obviously out for what she could get. A girl
who'd been far too young for him. He'd only considered
for a split second the clearly preposterous possibility that
what had actually bothered him was the fact that Javier had
seemed to be having so much fun being a fool.

On the day of the funeral she had looked much more
demure, but Raul had known what sort of woman lurked
behind the modest suit and sweetly sad expression. The few
tendrils of hair that had escaped the severe chignon had
been bright against the back of the slim-fitting suit she had

worn, the light application of blusher along her cheekbones had served to emphasise her extreme pallor.

Raul's expression hardened as he dragged his mind back to the present and his eyes back to her face. Someone lacking his knowledge of her history would have been unable to reconcile this unsophisticated figure before him with a young woman who had at eighteen cleverly inveigled her way into a recently bereaved man's home, bed and heart. To be able to disguise such ruthless self-interest behind a guileless façade would be truly an asset, he decided cynically.

'Miss Rose…'

Did she, he wondered, cultivate that candid and rather unnervingly direct blue gaze? He saw an expression of impatience flicker in the cornflower-blue eyes; his own eyes narrowed.

Raul was not unnerved, nor even intrigued by the wide-eyed stuff. His glance slid dismissively over the suggestion of slight curves beneath the voluminous nightgear. No doubt there were men whose chivalrous instincts were aroused by such fragility, but his instincts, protective or otherwise, were not excited by this style of delicate vulnerability.

'Keep your voice down,' she hissed, glancing over her shoulder.

Raul, unaccustomed to being on the other end of an order, stiffened in astonishment to hear the terse note of command in her low-pitched voice.

'Are the children ready?'

'No, they're not.' Nell smiled to take the sting out of her admission as she struggled to maintain her composure, at least outwardly.

Inside she did not have the luxury of pretence; the instant she had laid eyes on him standing there like some avenging angel on her doorstep every protective instinct she possessed had awoken. So had a lot of other instincts, but Nell couldn't see that dwelling on those was going to help the present situation.

She was frustrated by the inherent weakness responsible for her turbulent pulse-rate and unsteady hands, but not surprised by it. There was nothing subtle about what Raul Carreras oozed, unless you considered being hit over the head by a large blunt object subtle! And Nell seriously doubted if her response to his brand of raw sexuality made her in any way unique.

'I thought I had made my wishes clear.'

It was obvious from his tone that it had not for one second even crossed his mind that anyone would ignore an instruction he had given, no matter how misjudged said instruction might be.

'You did,' she agreed placidly. 'But I thought it wasn't a good idea,' she elaborated.

Raul stared at her. '*You* thought…?'

Was he outraged at the idea she could think, or the fact she had dared think something he didn't want her to? It was his expression of total astonishment that made her annoyance tip over into amusement.

Her grin produced a predictable gleam of awakening anger in his deep-set eyes—this was not a man to whom laughing at himself came easily. Nell arranged her features in a suitably sober expression. There was no point deliberately antagonising him and, she reminded herself, his night had been even more hellish than her own. Under the circumstances the guy was allowed not to be in the mood to party or even smile, she thought, studying his magnificently brooding profile. God, but he really was something extra special.

Being a fair-minded person, Nell knew that if he'd been

anyone else she'd have automatically cut him a bit of slack without a second thought. The problem was he wasn't anyone else. *The fact is,* she told herself, *you can't allow your judgement to be clouded by his sexual charisma.* You couldn't hold a man personally responsible for looking like your fantasy dream lover and then compounding the crime by ruining the illusion when he opened his mouth.

Maybe that was just as well, she reflected ruefully; if his personality had turned out to be as sublimely perfect as his raw, rampantly male looks, the fact he was totally unattainable to someone like herself would have been seriously tragic.

The thought of how unspeakably awful it must have been for him to think, even temporarily, that the children had been snatched brought a sympathetic warmth to her expression of which she was totally unaware as she read her hormones a firm lecture on self-control.

'Look, I really don't think you've thought this through,' she told him kindly. 'Why don't we talk about it? Would you like to come in?' She stepped a little to one side.

'There is nothing to *think through* and I should *like* to take the children back home in my car, which is no doubt being vandalised.'

His continued inexplicable antagonism was beginning to really niggle her. 'Oh, it's your *car* you're worried about.' She regretted the childish retort the moment it escaped her lips. 'And here was me thinking it was Kate and Antonio,' she finished in defiance of his glowering disapproval.

One strongly delineated dark brow lifted. 'Frankly, Miss Rose, I do not think my worries are any of *your* concern.' His fine nostrils quivered as he looked contemptuously down his patrician nose at her.

His dismissive attitude brought a flush to Nell's cheeks. For someone she associated with emotional detachment, here was something inescapably personal about the uncon-cealed contempt in his voice and manner.

A natural optimist, blessed with an easygoing nature, Nell had managed to go through life without making ene-mies. Finding herself on the receiving end of such hostility wasn't pleasant. Did he treat everyone this way or was she receiving special treatment? She didn't crave Raul Carreras's approval, but if his antipathy was personal it wasn't going to help her advocacy of the children's case.

'Kate and Antonio are my concern though.' The mystery was no longer why Katerina had run away from her uncle, but why it had taken her so long! Imagining her own fate in the hands of such a man sent a shiver down Nell's spine.

The grim smile that curved his wide, sensual mouth was without humour as he coldly replied, 'Thankfully that is not true.' Nell opened her mouth to contradict him, but was forestalled by his smooth and astonishing addition. 'You are my dead brother's ex-mistress, a position I think you'll find will carry very little weight legally or otherwise.'

Mistress!

Now the explanation for his attitude had revealed itself Nell didn't know why she was so astounded, or why this possibility hadn't occurred to her earlier. It wasn't as if this were the first time some ill-informed person had assumed Javier and she had been lovers.

Even though it seemed laughably preposterous to her, if she thought about it objectively Nell could see how they got there. They had shared a house, not had other partners and, despite the age gap, Javier had been a very attractive man, though not admittedly in the same class as his younger brother.

But then who was?

Nell scanned the lean, dark and permanently bad-tempered features of Raul Carreras from under the protec-

tive shield of her lashes. He might be an overbearing pain
but there was no denying the man really did have raw sex
appeal coming out of his pores. As gorgeous as he was to
look at, in Nell's eyes his staggering beauty didn't com
pensate for him being a humourless, stuck-up bully.

A thoughtful expression on her face, she tried to figure
out how he had come to the conclusion she and Javier had
been lovers. Though she had never personally met the man
up until the day of the funeral she did know that he and
Javier had met up infrequently. Nell could recall thinking
it was touching when she had learnt that Javier's younger
brother had broken ranks and did have contact with the
estranged member of the family.

Had Javier said something during one of their infrequent
meetings that his brother had misinterpreted? If he had real
ised, Javier, who had been *extremely* protective of her rep
utation, would no doubt have put him straight. Javier on
the surface, unorthodox and caring little for convention
actually never stopped being essentially a Spanish male
and as such he held some quaintly old-fashioned idea
about a woman's reputation. He had been much more con
cerned about what people might think than she had been.

As far as Nell herself was concerned the people that mat
tered knew the only interest Javier had in her was mildly
paternal, and, besides, the sort of people that thought ill o
her were not the sort of people she cared much about any
way.

'It has been a trying evening, Miss Rose. I think you'l
find it is imprudent to try my patience.'

Nell's dazed gaze focused openly on his dark face. Nell
didn't have much practice at hating but in that split second
as their eyes meshed the dislike she felt for him hardened
into something far more implacable than mere dislike. Rau

Carreras was not the sort of man who inspired tepid emotions.

Until that moment she had fully intended to set him straight, but that changed too. Her full mouth arranged itself into a mutinous line. Let him think what he liked; she didn't owe him any explanation.

'Is that a threat?' she enquired quietly.

'It is a statement of fact.'

'Will you lower your voice? I have neighbours, you know.'

'I would have thought that in an area such as this noise is the least of the neighbours' problems.' Every time Raul thought of the children walking through such an area in the middle of the night his blood ran cold.

'Why, you snob!' she exclaimed contemptuously.

A muscle clenched in his lean cheek as Raul studied her angry face with an air of baffled frustration. He ran a hand down the back of his sleek dark hair before rubbing it along the stubble that dusted his angular jawline.

'Would you be happy to walk alone here at night?'

'I have done.' No need to mention she had not done so out of choice and had been extremely uneasy.

'Then you are a fool,' he condemned.

No, just a liar. 'You're entitled to your opinion.' *And don't you enjoy sharing it?*

'I am willing to overlook your involvement in tonight's events,' he revealed in the manner of someone making a major concession. 'However, there are limits to my patience,' he revealed in a colourless, bored tone.

'*Involvement?*' she queried sharply. 'Listen, I realise having someone to blame means you don't have to examine your own behaviour, but I didn't volunteer to be your scapegoat.'

'I am not suggesting you planned what happened.'

Planned? Good God! Was that what he was thinking? 'That's *terribly* good of you,' she choked with leaden irony.

'You expect me to believe you didn't plant the idea in Katerina's head? Oh, I'm sure you were subtle,' he conceded nastily. 'A word here, a word there…' His eyes narrowed suspiciously. 'I don't know what you think you'll gain from exploiting the fondness my niece and nephew have for you? However, I think you should remember that I am not my brother.'

As if I'm likely to forget! 'You're suggesting?' Nell swallowed and shook her head, feeling the anger building steadily inside her.

'My brother obviously had a fondness for you, *I don't*,' he spelt out coldly. 'If these children come to any harm because of you, you will answer to me. Oh…' he smiled grimly into her pale face '…in case you were wondering, that *was* a threat.'

'You're suggesting that I encouraged them to run away?' Her voice rose to a shrill pitch, which made him wince. 'I'd really like to be around when you realise just how much you've underestimated Katerina.' And if he was half as patronising to the teenager as he was with her he wouldn't have to wait long, she thought grimly.

'Do not try and deflect the blame,' he recommended scornfully.

'I'm not!' Nell exclaimed angrily. 'I just meant that you don't begin to appreciate just how resourceful and bright Katerina is.' *Or how much she needs someone to love her,* she thought sadly.

'I am aware that Katerina is an intelligent child; however,' he added disapprovingly, 'she lacks focus.'

'She didn't lack focus when she knocked out your security.' Nell watched a look of genuine shock chase across his dark, devastating features.

'*Katerina?*' Raul, scepticism etched on his lean, dark features, shook his head. 'It is not possible.'

Nell smiled and Raul's jaw tightened.

'I blame myself for not putting a stop to the phone calls and e-mails.' He placed a hand on the doorjamb above her head.

Hot with hating, Nell lifted her shimmering eyes to his and without warning was submerged by a wave of enervating lust so intense she couldn't breathe. It hurt; it physically hurt. Nell, unable to tear her eyes from Raul's face, couldn't have said whether she was standing, sitting or lying down. Praying for things to return to normal, she fought to control her rising panic.

It was the cringe-inducing possibility that he was not unaware of the effect his physical closeness had on her that enabled Nell to assume an attitude of defiance even when his voice dropped to a soft, threatening murmur that made the hairs on her nape stand on end.

'But I intend to rectify that error.'

'By allowing me no contact with them? You wouldn't be that cruel?' The sweat that had broken out on the surface of her skin was cooling; it wasn't a nice feeling.

She watched one dark brow lift to a satiric angle.

'Your confidence in my essential kindness is flattering, but misplaced.'

'That's nothing to boast about,' she remonstrated tartly.

There was a fulminating silence punctuated by the sound of his inhalation.

'It is clear to me,' Raul added in an icy voice, 'that without your influence they would have settled down into their new life by now.'

Nell regarded him with open incredulity. 'Not even *you* can believe that.'

'Certainly I believe that,' he rebutted from between clenched teeth.

Was it her imagination or was that a defensive note she was hearing in his voice?

'How can they recover when you are constantly raking up the past?' he said harshly.

'You mean I talk about their father? They need to talk about him. *I* need to talk about him,' she added huskily. She turned her head away, blinking furiously as she felt her eyes flood with sudden tears. When she felt she had regained enough control to meet his gaze she discovered he was looking at her with a bewildering, angry intensity.

'They can talk about Javier to me.'

'You didn't know him.' Nell heard his harsh intake of breath and gave a penitent grimace. 'Not that that was really your fault.'

'Save your empathy; I'm not about to change my mind. It's obvious that you exert a considerable and undesirable influence on the children.'

'You're calling me undesirable?'

'Undesirable...?'

Something in his voice, something she couldn't quite pin down, made her study his face with extra attention. She watched his long jet lashes lift from his incredible eyes and for a split second their eyes locked. The white heat in his eyes made Nell recoil. She was totally unconscious of the tiny gasp that escaped her parted lips.

'Just take me to the children,' he rasped.

Nell barely registered him brush past her as she continued to stare blankly at the space he had occupied moments earlier. Despite the core of heat low in her belly, she shivered. Primitive and explicitly sexual—the look in his incredible eyes had been both, and it had been directed at her! They said hate and love were closely related; perhaps the same could be said for hate and lust?

CHAPTER FOUR

IT WAS a little while before the suffocating excitement had receded enough for Nell to regain control of herself. She walked into the flat and found all but one of the doors leading off the sitting room open; Raul had his hand on the handle of the one that still remained closed.

'What do you think you're—? You can't go in there!' She caught him by the arm but wasn't quick enough to stop him pushing open the door into her bedroom. His impetuous stride stilled as he saw the two children asleep on the bed, Antonio under the covers and Katerina lying on top with Nell's dressing gown and a fleece throw arranged over her sleeping figure.

Raul froze; Nell saw his chest rise as he inhaled sharply. His head turned towards her and as their eyes met her own hand fell self-consciously from his arm. His expression was unreadable as he turned and stared at the sleeping children. How, she wondered, did you take the measure of a man who hid his feelings so well? Well, not *always*, she thought, recalling with a shudder the raw hunger she had glimpsed in his eyes.

She held her breath as he reached down, imagining he was going to rouse the sleeping children, but instead he pulled the quilt Antonio had half kicked off up to the sleeping boy's chin; his hand hovered above the child's flushed cheek but he didn't touch him. The tenderness in the unexpected action caught Nell totally unawares. She turned abruptly and left the room alarmed by the swell of emotion that made her chest tight.

She closed her eyes and leaned against the wall. One thing was obvious—he did care about the children, he just didn't have the faintest idea how to show it. When she opened them she found he had joined her.

'Why didn't you simply tell me they were asleep?' he demanded, raking her with an accusing glare.

Nell released an incredulous gasp. 'What do you think I was trying to do? I had assumed,' she continued sarcastically, 'that by the time you'd got here you'd have realised it was totally impractical, not to mention cruel, to drag them across London at this time of night.'

His expression did not alter as their combative glances locked, but there were faint dark bands of colour across the slashing contours of his cheekbones that suggested her words had found their mark.

'Almost as cruel as to encourage them to stage this dangerous stunt in the first case, perhaps?'

'Not that again!' she exclaimed with an exasperated groan.

The muscles in his jaw clenched. 'Did they tell you they couldn't talk to me?'

Nell guessed the question had cost him a lot in the pride department. This was probably as close to humble as he got. It really was the height of foolishness to start feeling sorry for him, she remonstrated with herself angrily. 'You could try listening to what they say once in a while.'

He visibly bit back an indignant response. Lean features rigid, he turned his back on her. Nell watched from under the sweep of her lashes as he rolled his head, flexing the powerful muscles of his neck and shoulders to relieve the tension there. Her stomach muscles quivered. When her knees showed an alarming tendency to shake she perched on the edge of the sofa arm.

'They were unhappy enough to run away.' It wasn't

a question; it was a statement of fact. 'Did they tell you why?'

'I don't think Antonio is unhappy.'

He responded to her attempt to be tactful by slinging her a look of simmering impatience over his shoulder before presenting her once more with his broad back. 'But Katerina is?'

'She's worried that you're going to send Antonio away to school,' Nell admitted. 'She feels responsible for him.'

Raul turned back to face her, his hand still massaging the back of his neck. 'She's too young to feel responsible for anyone.'

Nell sighed and shook her head in agreement. 'Do you *have* to separate them?'

'Everything is arranged; it is a very good school. I went there myself.' There was an ironic twist to his lips as his dark eyes scanned her face. 'I realise that that might not be much of a recommendation as far as you're concerned...as it helped make me the man I am today.'

An unwilling laugh was drawn from Nell. 'I doubt you were ever that malleable.'

Despite her words an image of small, solitary figure packed off to boarding-school in a foreign country entered her head. It was hard to visualise this strong, confident man ever suffering the traumas of growing up. Raul was one of those people you couldn't imagine ever being a child—despite this, the image of the lonely boy lingered in her head.

'I'm sure you had an excellent education and it made you self-sufficient and all that stuff, but were you happy? Did you actually enjoy your time there?'

'Their father went there also, though by the time I arrived he had left. However,' Raul added drily, 'his reputation remained.'

Javier had been a legend: a popular head boy and a talented sportsman whose captaincy of the school teams had filled the trophy cabinets. It had been made clear to Raul within minutes of his arrival at the prestigious school that great things had been expected of him.

Raul had been a great disappointment to those who had been hoping for him to step into his brother's shoes.

Ironically, considering that it had been Javier who had later opted out of the path people had expected him to follow, it had been the younger brother who had been unable to accept authority while at school. His dangerously seditious tendencies had been noted and deplored. He had been quickly labelled a loner, and, even worse in the British public school system, not a team player! His total indifference to the approval of his peers or authority had quickly set him apart. If it had not been for his undisputed academic brilliance Raul would have been considered a failure by the system.

Head on one side, Nell regarded the tall, enigmatic figure with narrow-eyed speculation. He had avoided answering her question—was that significant? She decided there was nothing to be lost from pressing the point.

'You pulled strings to get Antonio into this school?' Almost imperceptibly, he nodded. 'Couldn't you pull some more and *unarrange* it? Or at least delay making any final decisions just yet?' she suggested tentatively.

He exhaled noisily and folded his rangy frame into her overstuffed chintz-covered armchair. The action bore the same hallmarks of unstudied elegance that typified even his simplest action. Nell, whose feet were drawn to stray banana skins, watched enviously. He couldn't have been clumsy even if he tried, she thought.

'You think that I should give in to a stunt like this?' He leaned forward, extracted a cushion from behind his back and dropped it on the floor with an expression of masculine distaste before settling himself back again. 'What sort of message will that send out?' he demanded.

Nell responded to this reasonable question with a shake of her head.

Raul pressed his point. 'If I cave in this time, the next time I make a decision that Katerina doesn't like she'll think all she has to do is run off. I'm not going to be held to ransom by a teenager.'

'That's the point, isn't it? She is a teenager. This isn't a terrorist gang you're dealing with, it's children. Confused, frightened children. Saying this family doesn't negotiate isn't a solution.'

Raul ran a hand over the stubble along his jaw-line and fixed her with an unfriendly stare. 'Then what is the solution?' he demanded in a clipped tone.

'Why are you asking me?'

'Well, you're the one with all the answers. The *sweet* voice of reason.'

His sardonic tone brought a flush of angry colour to her cheeks.

'Well, *someone* has to be,' she bit back. 'And to tell you the truth I'm just about sick of it. You're as bad as Katerina!' she condemned angrily. 'But at least *she* has got the excuse of being fifteen and the victim of rioting hormones. I warn you, if *you* lock yourself in the bathroom and start bawling I shan't be offering you a shoulder to cry on. I didn't ask to be piggy-in-the-middle, you know,' she finished on a note of breathless indignation.

Raul's glance dropped from her stormy, flushed face to her heaving bosom, then back. Holding her eyes, he stretched his long, long legs in front of him and dug his hands into his pockets. Nothing could have been more languid than his body language, but Nell wasn't fooled; Raul wasn't the sort of man who would tolerate anyone berating him lying down.

The silence between them stretched, punctuated only by her audible respiration as she fought to catch her breath.

'I have hormones...' His voice had a seductively abrasive quality.

'Congratulations.'

His dark lashes swept upwards from the high curve of his sculpted cheeks. 'But none of them are urging me to lock myself in your bathroom.'

Her heart skipped several beats. Nell definitely didn't want him to tell her what his hormones were urging him to do.

'Shall we leave your hormones out of this?' she suggested with a grimace of distaste. The problem was that the distaste was feigned. Actually she was excited—deeply, *disastrously* excited.

'Certainly. If they make you uncomfortable?'

She longed to wipe that complacent smirk off his face. 'Wasn't that the idea?' she challenged. 'Listen, I'm perfectly prepared to admit you're a very attractive man, but you're simply not my type.'

As he angled a look at her flushed face his disbelief was palpable and predictable; Raul Carreras had probably never been knocked back in his life.

'Then what is your type?'

'*My type?*' she parroted vaguely. His dark eyes had a dangerously hypnotic quality; looking into those silver-shot depths she felt a little light-headed and hot—*very hot*. Nell's response was inspired by a combination of desperation and instinct.

'Javier.'

It worked.

In the blink of an eye all expression was wiped clear of

Raul's face. 'How could I have forgotten?' he drawled icily.

'Compromise isn't a dirty word, you know,' she rushed on huskily. 'There are no easy solutions, but it might help if you actually asked the children what they want. What's so funny?' she demanded as his white teeth were revealed in a cynical grin.

'I was trying to imagine my father asking me what I wanted.'

'The idea is to learn from our parents' mistakes, not emulate them.'

Raul was on his feet in one lithe, fluid motion. 'And you feel qualified to comment on my parents because…?' He sounded deceptively soft, but his true feelings were revealed by the expression of hard disdain etched on his lean features as he glared down at her from his full, threatening height.

Nell coloured, but remained composed beneath his crushing contempt. It wasn't easy. 'Your father never met his grandchildren.'

Her perceptive observation made him freeze. The smile that thinned his sensual lips was ironic. *'Touché.'*

Nell lowered her gaze. There was something addictive about watching him, the way he moved, his facial expressions, even the angle of his head. They all held an unhealthy fascination for her.

'However, I am *not* my father.' His lean body quivered with an invisible tension.

Oh, God! She'd only just resolved to keep her involvement with Raul Carreras to the bare minimum. She'd offer advice in an objective and unemotional way. There would be no more emotional outbursts, personal comments or waves of uncontrollable burning lust—especially no lust!

Despite this resolution she couldn't keep her curiosity in check as she looked at the tall figure glaring at her.

So things hadn't been easy between Raul and his father.

'I wish you'd sit down; you're very intimidating towering over me like that.'

To her relief the hauteur faded from Raul's face as he glared down at her. He released a short, bitter laugh. 'You're not intimidated by me,' he accused.

Nell, who was more than happy for him to carry on thinking that way, smiled. 'Do you want me to be?'

He ground his teeth audibly in frustration. 'I want—! I want you to...' *I want you. 'Dios mío!'*

'There's no need to raise your voice.' There was something alarming about his rigid posture. 'Are you all right?'

Raul dragged a hand through his dark glossy hair before turning his head. His expression was cloaked as their eyes met. He gave a tight smile.

'It would seem you have won. I will allow the children to sleep.'

'It wasn't a contest.'

'No?' He shrugged. 'Either way I think I should be going.' He consulted the metal-banded watch on his wrist and his brows rose when he saw the hour. 'What time shall I pick up the children?'

Despite the cold formality of his question, Nell felt irrationally protective as he dragged his hair back from his face with his hand—the gesture was so incredibly weary.

Feeling protective of Raul Carreras? Well, I can't blame that on my frustrated maternal instincts, she thought as her greedy glance made a surreptitious survey of his lean, powerfully developed body. It was probably the air of vigour that was an intrinsic part of him that had made her miss the tell-tale signs of exhaustion in his face earlier.

Faint shadows beneath his deep-set eyes, a pallor underlying the natural healthy glow of his dark-toned skin and lines of tension bracketing his mouth all suggested it had been some time since he'd seen his bed—*his own, anyway*.

Don't go there, Nell, she silently warned herself.

Well, even if his debauched lifestyle was responsible for his fatigue it didn't alter the fact it would be foolish to let him needlessly drive across the city.

'By the time you get home it will almost be time for you to come back,' she observed.

He looked at her sharply. A furrow appeared between his dark brows. 'Are you suggesting I don't go?' he asked softly.

His tone made her flush; she swallowed. 'I'm saying that if you would prefer to use my sofa you're welcome.'

He looked around her small, cramped sitting room. 'And where will you sleep?'

'Not with you.'

'I always think it's wiser to wait until you're asked.'

Under his mocking stare the pinkness of her face deepened to a bright crimson, which she knew clashed with her hair. 'I'm trying to be nice to you, despite the fact you've been perfectly horrid to me since the moment you arrived,' she choked. 'And all you can do is make fun of me. The fact is you look terrible.' *In a beautiful and darkly devastating sort of way.* 'You'll probably drive into a lamp post and kill yourself. I don't want to feel responsible for that.'

He regarded her as though she were a strange species he had never come across before.

'If I thought I was unsafe I would not drive.'

Nell gave a bitter laugh. 'The majority of men who drink and drive actually think that alcohol improves their skills.'

The muscles along his jaw tightened. 'You accuse me! *Por Dios.* I do not drink and drive!' Raul breathed, pinning her with an outraged stare.

'I wasn't suggesting you did. The point I was trying to make is what you *think* you're capable of and what you actually are capable of may not be the same thing.'

Raul did not look mollified by her hasty explanation. 'These men who drink alcohol and get behind the wheel also probably think a few pints also improves their performance in bed,' he observed scornfully. 'I find it offensive to be compared with such men.'

'I think,' she replied drily, 'that you've established that. I was simply suggesting you might be more tired than you think and just offering you a bed for what is left of the night,' she said, wishing she'd not bothered. 'I'm not suggesting you don't know your limits in bed or out!' She closed her eyes. *Oh, God, did I really say that?*

'There are occasions when I surprise even myself.'

Oh, yes, I really did say it!

She took a deep breath and opened her eyes, all her efforts concentrated on not letting her mind go back to the place where it was imagining what Raul was capable of in bed.

'Look,' she snapped, meeting his eyes defiantly. 'Do you want to stay or not?'

'Stay.'

Her stomach lurched somewhere below her knees. *Well, you asked him,* she told herself unsympathetically. 'Right.' She slowly counted to ten. 'No problem. I'll get a blanket and pillow.'

'No need. I'll take the chair.' He nodded towards the chintzy number. 'You have the sofa.'

'That's stupid, you're too tall.' She eyed his six-feet-five frame with as much objectivity as she was capable of.

'We could share?' he suggested.

'If you're going to be facetious…' she croaked as a wave of debilitating heat washed over her body.

There was no humour in the look he sent back. 'I appreciate a frank exchange of views as much as anyone, but do you have to turn everything into an argument?'

'That's rich coming from…' She stopped as he began to shrug off his jacket. His actions followed by her disbelieving eyes, he then proceeded to slip the top button of his shirt before responding in a tone that did not invite discussion.

'I'll take the chair.'

The subject of where they should sleep no longer seemed so vitally important to Nell. Her tense glance kept flickering from his face to the section of bare, lean golden torso—a section that was getting larger and larger with each passing second.

'What are you doing?' she asked.

'I'm taking off my clothes.'

'I can see that!' His skin was an even golden all over—at least everywhere she could see. There was a light dusting of dark hair across his chest, which was broad. There was not an ounce of excess flesh to hide the well-defined but non-bulky musculature of his upper body. Perfect was an overused term but in this case it seemed frankly inadequate to describe how better than good his body was.

If he was aware of her scrutiny it didn't seem to bother him. 'Then why did you ask?'

Nell opened her mouth to reply, saw him unfasten the belt around his trim, lean belly and changed her mind. She literally ran to the airing cupboard in the bathroom, yanked out all the spare blankets she had, ran back into the room, threw half of them at him and switched off the light. She climbed into her own makeshift bed fully clothed.

It was a little while before the sounds of Raul settling down stopped.

'Sleep well, Nell Rose.'

The amusement in his deep voice made her bring her teeth together in jarring impact. Of course he knew she wouldn't sleep. He knew she would lie there in the dark, a bundle of lustful longing.

In the darkness she scrunched up her face in a mortified grimace. How could you be so obvious? Acting like a scared idiot who had never seen a man semi-clothed before.

'Goodnight,' she replied coolly.

The other side of the room Raul heard the moment her breathing changed and became deep and regular. He didn't sleep.

CHAPTER FIVE

NELL opened her eyes. 'Hello,' she said, stretching sleepily like a cat. One arm still curled above her head, she smiled.

Raul caught his breath at the sleepy invitation in the long-lashed china-blue eyes.

'What are you doing?'

The shrill accusation in Katerina's voice succeeded in severing Nell's link with the dream world. She jerked upright, her eyes wide, her mouth half open, gasping for air like someone who had just been immersed in icy water.

'I...I was dreaming...' For a moment there—a dangerous moment—subconscious and conscious, dreams and reality had clashed.

'Your eyes were open.'

Raul straightened up with far less haste. Without any sign of self-consciousness he began to button up his shirt. 'Good morning, Katerina,' he said to his niece.

'What are you doing here?' she snarled, bristling with suspicion. 'And what,' she added with a pointed glare in Nell's direction that shrieked *traitor*, 'are you doing with Nell?' Her lip curled. 'Like I need to ask...'

Ridiculously Nell felt guilty. 'Your uncle stayed because by the time we'd finished there was no point in him going home and coming back,' she explained, having no intention of responding to the youngster's suspicions.

'Finishing doing what?'

Raul's eyes moved from Nell's red face to Katerina's defiant one.

'Keep a civil tongue in your head.' He delivered this

instruction with blighting scorn. 'You are in no position to comment on anyone else's conduct after your behaviour, especially someone who has gone out of her way to help you.'

Nell saw the colour rise in Katerina's face. Although the girl had too much pride to back down, she felt a sharp spasm of sympathy for her.

'Kate didn't mean anything...' Her intervention was totally disregarded by the two combatants.

'Wake your brother and we will leave. Miss Rose has been put to enough inconvenience on our behalf already.' Nell watched him extract a mobile phone from his pocket and toss it towards the teenager who automatically caught it. His stony expression would have daunted anyone, let alone a young girl. 'Ring your grandmother to tell her you are all right; the sedation the doctor gave her should have worn off by now.'

As if she doesn't feel guilty enough already, Nell thought angrily.

Katerina looked at her uncle, her eyes filling with tears, before she turned and stomped back into the bedroom.

Nell dealt the tall, intimidating figure an exasperated frown. 'Did you *have* to speak to her that way?'

Raul looked at her blankly. 'What way?'

Nell clutched her hair in both hands and groaned. 'My God, you really are no great loss to the world of diplomacy, are you? Couldn't you *try* and be conciliatory?' *Silly question, Nell,* she thought, allowing her eyes to travel the length of his tall, striking figure—*conciliatory* wasn't even in his vocabulary.

'She spoke to you with disrespect.'

Nell looked at him—no, he wasn't being ironic. 'For someone who can't open his mouth without insulting me, that's pretty farcical.'

Their eyes meshed and for what seemed like a long time to Nell he didn't say anything. When he did his words were totally unexpected.

'You smiled at me.' His manner was atypically distracted and there was a faint accusatory note in his voice.

'Is that a crime?' She gave a provoked sigh. 'Like I said, I was half asleep; I was dreaming.'

'Was I in your dream?' His low, husky drawl had an intimate quality.

Nell blinked to break the mesmeric hold of his eyes. 'It was a dream, not a nightmare,' she rasped huskily.

Her spikiness drew a wolfish grin from him.

Eyes still on his face, she pulled herself into a cross-legged position. 'Listen,' she began in a low, urgent voice. 'I know you don't think much of me or my advice, but go easy on Katerina. She's a good girl, and she won't abuse your trust if you do.'

For a moment he stared down expressionlessly into her earnest features. His lips formed a twisted smile. 'You really care about them, don't you?'

Before Nell had time to ask why he should find that so amazing a small figure emerged from the bedroom. And when he saw his uncle a visible sigh of relief ran through Antonio's thin frame.

For Nell it was a very revealing moment. She realised that her impression the previous evening, gained from a few sleepy comments that Antonio had made, had been correct. Antonio was not unhappy with his new guardian; Antonio's participation in this was about loyalty to his sister.

'You're here.'

'I am.'

'Are you going to take us home?'

'Do you want me to?' Raul squatted down to child height.

Antonio considered the question gravely. 'I think we need someone to look after us. Kate thinks she can but she's just a girl. I tried to tell her, but…'

Silently Raul held open his arms and the little boy ran into them. Nell felt her throat thicken emotionally as the child was enfolded in a tight embrace. Raul stood up holding the boy in his arms; he looked at Nell over the child's dark head and saw the glimmer of tears in her china-blue eyes.

'I think Katerina might miss you if you went away. What would you feel, Antonio, about going to a school closer to home for a while?' He set the boy down on the floor and looked at him enquiringly.

'Live with you, you mean…all the time?'

Raul nodded. 'If you wouldn't mind.'

'Kate…Kate!' Her brother's excited cries brought Katerina running into the room.

'What's wrong?'

'I'm not going away to school. I'm going to stay with you.'

'Really?' She looked suspiciously at her uncle who inclined his head fractionally in affirmation. There was a pause. 'Thank you. I know you wouldn't be doing this if Nell hadn't made you,' she revealed. 'But thank you anyhow.'

Nell's embarrassment was profound. 'I couldn't make your uncle do anything he didn't want to,' she corrected hastily.

She slid a sideways look at Raul's austere profile to see how he was taking the news of being putty in her hands and was relieved to see the suggestion hadn't sent him hurtling into outraged 'nobody tells me what to do' macho mode.

'Miss Rose underestimates her powers of persuasion.'

This smooth observation startled her.

'And if we both *wanted* the same thing…' There was an inescapably sensual message in the slow sweep of his sloe-dark eyes as they moved up her body.

It took a couple of seconds for her to get his drift and when she did Nell blushed to the roots of her hair. She pointedly turned her back on Raul but, despite the symbolic gesture of dismissal, her traitorous body still hummed with the desire he had evoked just by looking.

God help me if he takes it into his head to do more than look!

She worried when she reviewed the events later that she might have seemed a bit too eager to get them out of the door, but hopefully the youngsters, on a promise of breakfast at the nearest fast-food outlet, hadn't noticed.

If Raul himself had noticed it didn't matter because she was going to make a point of *not* seeing him again.

CHAPTER SIX

THE representative from the local authority was sympathetic, but made it clear there would be no last-minute reprieve for the centre. The authority's resources, he explained, were already stretched thin on the ground, and art therapy for children with physical and learning difficulties, while admirable, was considered in the present climate a luxury they could no longer afford.

The staff and parents who had come to the meeting to plead their case decided to go to the pub to drown their collective sorrows. Nell, who didn't feel in the mood for company, or a smoke-filled bar, offered to stay behind to clear away the chairs and tea things.

While she worked her thoughts were focused on the problem in hand. Not a person to give up easily, she refused to believe the situation was hopeless. Despite her natural optimism, when the last of the teacups was washed and the final chair stacked, she still hadn't been visited by a blinding flash of inspiration. Maybe the others were right; maybe it was time to call it a day?

Feeling pretty disconsolate, she picked up her bag. It was then she noticed a few items from earlier that day that hadn't been returned to the store cupboard. Her innately tidy nature made it impossible for her to leave them where they were.

Nell was reaching up, straining to replace a bundle of brushes to the top shelf where they were stored, when they were taken from her grasp and placed on the shelf.

She let out a startled yelp and spun around only to find herself face to chest with Raul Carreras.

A lean hand shot out to steady her as she stepped backwards straight into the sharp corner of a low shelf.

'Are you hurt?'

Even when Nell had shrugged off his steadying hand the warm imprint remained. 'No, I'm fine...fine,' she babbled brightly through a miasma of pain. At least the stabbing pain in her thigh had halted the dragging sexual inertia, startling in its capacity to disconnect her brain from her body, that she had felt inexorably stealing over her in those few seconds of eye contact.

'Did I startle you?'

Startled hardly covered the state of total chaos her nervous system had been plunged into. Nell pressed a hand to her throat as her eyes slid helplessly over the long, lean, powerful frame of the man who had occupied her thoughts more than was healthy during the last week. At times, his spending the night on her sofa had seemed like an invention of her overactive imagination.

This unreality went double for the night the evening news had splashed images of him all over her television screen. Images of him looking quite incredibly handsome at a sparkling film première, with the equally sparkling young female star of the film clinging to him like a second skin.

Raul's hands had covered more flesh than the star's outfit had! To be fair, Raul's dark, dramatic looks had attracted just as much attention as the daring, and to Nell's mind totally tasteless, designer dress his companion had *almost* been wearing.

The next day the tabloids had been filled with photos of the impossibly attractive couple along with endless speculation about a rumoured forthcoming engagement between the divorced actress and the wealthy financier.

Unlike the rest of the country's adult population Nell had no interest whatsoever in Raul's wedding plans. She didn't care which designer would be entrusted to make the bride's wedding dress and had no interest whatever in which celebrities might be on the guest list.

It had only been a very natural concern for what his impending nuptials might mean for Antonio and Katerina that had made her scour the tabloids for information. This concern was the reason that her own reaction to a suggested spring wedding had been less over the moon than the fashion editors'.

The pretty actress might be a mother-earth type, with maternal instincts coming out of her ears, but if she wasn't she wouldn't be exactly overjoyed having two children around. As for Raul, his girlfriend looked more than capable of making him forget his responsibilities.

Nell had tried very hard not to dwell on what methods the nubile young actress might employ to induce amnesia, or on whether she was *quite* so personally disinterested as she kept telling herself. Now, of course, with him standing there, she knew her latter doubt was more than justified!

Could any woman be disinterested in a man like this?

Today the tuxedo Raul had been wearing at the film première had been replaced by more casual gear, casual but not cheap. The leather jacket alone probably cost enough to keep Nell's doomed charity project going until Christmas! Though, she admitted ruefully, he would have looked incredible in a brown paper bag, though perhaps not as sleekly dangerous as he did in black leather.

In the confined space she was acutely aware of the exclusive fragrance he wore, but more disturbing was the warm male scent that mingled with it. While she was getting a nose full of designer smell and pheromones he was no doubt being treated to the turpentine she had spilt earlier; perhaps that explained his sour expression.

'Did you startle me?' She tucked a strand of bright hair behind one ear, shook the rest of her shoulder-length mane back from her face and gave a dry laugh. 'You could say that.' Her expression hardened. 'Of course you did. What did you expect, creeping up like that?' she demanded tartly. 'You nearly gave me a heart attack!' She clasped her hand to the region where her heart was trying to batter its way out of her ribcage.

Raul's eyes followed her action; his mouth twisted sceptically. 'I suspect your heart is tougher than that,' he observed drily.

Serve him right if I dropped dead at his feet, she thought viciously. 'So now you're the medical expert, too?'

'I did call out, but you didn't hear me.'

She saw his eyes slide down the length of her jean-clad figure. Nell caught herself wishing that she had worn her new jeans, the hipsters that showed just a little bit of flat midriff, and was both shocked and ashamed. She liked to look nice, but she wasn't into competing for male approval, considering it both demeaning and pathetic.

On a more practical level, when the male in question was Raul Carreras who dated models and A-list actresses it was also a waste of time. You could dress up a sparrow but at the end of the day it was still a sparrow—or so her gran had been fond of saying.

'You couldn't have called out very loud,' she observed with a sniff. 'How did you find me anyhow?' she added, panic making her demand emerge aggressively.

'How do you know I was looking for you?' Raul countered, a mocking smile tugging at the corners of his mobile mouth as his dark eyes continued to scan her face—Raul was not one of those people who had a problem with eye contact, unfortunately.

'Well, I can't think of any other reason you'd be here.' *And, my goodness, I wish you weren't!*

The store room was actually pretty large and more than capable of accommodating two people, but when one of those people was Raul Carreras a barn would be too small. She made a conscious effort to slow her rapid inhalation. If she carried on hyperventilating she'd end up passing out—something she prided herself on never having done— or with her head in a brown paper bag!

Raul looked around the neatly stacked shelves of the store cupboard, his dark brows pleated. 'What is this place?'

'We store stuff here.'

'We?'

'I work for a charity that runs an art therapy course for children with learning difficulties.'

'So this is charity work?'

'Some people volunteer their services, but I'm a paid employee.' Though paid very little, so little in fact that she was forced to supplement her income working in a convenience store, but she doubted the state of her finances would interest him.

'And these children paint pictures?'

'Amongst other things,' she returned shortly. 'I'll spare you the details.'

'When I require sparing I will tell you,' he countered languidly. 'And you enjoy this work?'

'Why shouldn't I?' she demanded belligerently, then, before he had an opportunity to reply, continued. 'I suppose it seems flaky to you, but actually learning to express themselves through art and music can really help some of these children.' The frustration she had been successfully keeping in check all evening spilled over. 'But don't worry,' she added in a shaking voice, 'we won't be here long. Our grant has been withdrawn and by Christmas there won't be enough money to keep it going.'

He was staring at her, and small wonder, she thought suddenly, deeply embarrassed by her emotional outburst.

'You are upset about losing your job?'

A hissing sound of exasperation escaped through Nell's clenched teeth. 'You've totally missed the point, haven't you? Though I don't know why I expected anything else from someone like you,' she mumbled.

'Then why don't you tell me what the point is?' he suggested. Despite his mild tone Nell found there was a disturbing quality to his scrutiny. 'Preferably in words of one syllable that *someone like me* might understand.'

'This may look like a scruffy tin hut to you but to the children that come here, and their parents…' She broke off as tears began to seep from her eyes.

With a muttered curse she groped in her pocket for a tissue. The search produced a till receipt for her sandwich at lunchtime and a drawing that Tommy had done for her earlier that day. She knew she shouldn't have favourites, but Tommy was special. She unfolded the portrait of herself in blue crayon.

Raul watched the quivering movement of her lower lip and inwardly groaned. He could deal with Nell Rose, manipulative man-eater with no scruples, but a Nell Rose who gave every appearance of being a crusading do-gooder with attitude was another thing!

Either the woman had weird tendencies or he had miscalculated. Who was he kidding? Of course he had miscalculated. He'd known that for the last week; he'd just been too stubborn to admit it.

Why?

Nell Rose being his brother's mistress for financial gain was a situation he was more comfortable with than Nell Rose being his brother's mistress because she loved him. This insight raised a lot more questions than it answered, and Raul, who was not into soul-searching, was in no mood to consider what they might be.

Having finally discovered a tissue tucked up her sleeve, Nell blew her nose defiantly.

'Madre Mia!' He gave a heavy sigh of resignation and took a step towards the dejected figure with the pink-tipped nose. His attention fixed on the weeping girl, he didn't notice the bare bulb that illuminated the store room until he walked straight into it. He let out a grunt of pain as the light swung upwards and hit the ceiling.

Nell heard a gentle popping sound in the second before the lights went out. An ink-black darkness enveloped them.

'Don't move.'

Nell nodded, then realised that he couldn't see her.

'I wasn't going to.'

'I think the lights have fused.' His voice was closer now, so close she could hear his breathing and feel the warmth that came from his body. If she stretched out her hand she would probably touch him, even accidentally collide with him. The thought of leaning in close to all that hard maleness sent a rush of heat sweeping through her body. She caught her breath.

'Are you all right?'

'Fine.' Her reply emerged as a husky whisper.

The problem was the dark. There was something very dangerous about darkness. Fantasies fed on darkness: it freed up your imagination; it made you reckless, and it gave you a false sense of anonymity. It was easy to understand why people did things with the lights out that they wouldn't dream of doing with them on.

'Where is it, then?' he asked as though they both hadn't spent the last sixty seconds or so just breathing.

'Where is what?'

'The fuse-box.'

Nell told him and heard him move away. With him went the tension; it slid from her body leaving her limp. Carefully she felt her way out of the box-like room. The darkness in the main area of the warehouse was not as dense as it had been in the windowless store room.

Nell felt the solid wood of a workbench just as the lights went back on. She exhaled, deeply grateful that there were no embarrassing lapses in judgement for her to cringe about. It had been a close thing, though.

'Why do you assume that I would think your work here is of no value?' a soft voice at her elbow demanded.

Nell, who hadn't heard his soft-footed approach, started. 'Well, we don't make any money. There is no profit margin.' She turned her head and fixed him with a resentful glare. 'That's the way you measure things, isn't it?'

'I make money—that is what I do, and I see no reason to apologise for it.'

'And trample over people in the process!' she accused huskily.

The fine network of lines around his penetrating dark eyes deepened as they narrowed. 'Would you care to cite a specific example of my callous behaviour? I try not to judge people by the job they do or the clothes they wear and the car they drive.'

This censure struck Nell as the height of hypocrisy. She drew herself to her full, unimpressive height and wished not for the first time that she had been granted an extra few inches. In her experience people were a lot less likely to be patronising if you were tall and leggy.

'No, just on the person's bed they supposedly share.'

His jaw tightened. 'That was different.'

'Wow! You can say that with a straight face—I'm impressed.'

He shrugged. 'If I am guilty of prejudice, I am sorry.'

'*If!*'

'However,' he continued, ignoring her sarcastic interjection, 'it seems to me you are not without your own preconceptions. Making money automatically precludes me from the enjoyment of a piece of music?' He picked up a guitar that was propped up against the wall and strummed a soft chord. 'Or a fine painting, or even,' he added, lifting his eyes from the instrument he held, 'appreciating a person who has a vocation.'

'Point taken,' she grunted reluctantly. 'And appreciation makes a nice change from contempt.'

Raul, apparently satisfied that he had made his point placed the guitar back against the wall; a piece of plaster fell down as he did so. 'This place is in an appalling condition,' he observed, running his finger along the cracked window-pane with a fastidious frown. 'That fuse-box is prehistoric.'

Nell immediately felt defensive at this attack on the old building.

'And,' he went on, 'the security is non-existent. Anyone could have walked in.'

'And you did; aren't I the lucky one?'

Her flippant comment brought his disapproving attention zeroing in on her face. 'This is not a laughing matter.'

For some reason he seemed determined to make a drama out of a simple lapse of memory—she had meant to lock the door after the others had left. Nell sighed, irritated by his preoccupation with security.

'I was going to lock up when I left,' she explained, jangling the bunch of keys she had clipped to her belt.

'So you thought it perfectly reasonable to stay alone in n unlocked building. Don't you have any sense of self-reservation?' he demanded.

'I'm sure you didn't come here to discuss the security.'

'No.'

Her feathery brows lifted. 'Then…?' she prompted.

'You have not contacted Katerina and Antonio this veek.'

'Is that a question or are you monitoring their calls?'

He looked at her with exasperation. 'Do you *have* to be onfrontational?' He ran a hand through his sleek dark hair. I was simply wondering why you hadn't contacted them.'

'I thought you'd be pleased.'

'I didn't think my pleasure was of such importance to ou.'

She met his dark, mocking eyes and gritted her teeth. It's not high on my list of priorities,' she responded with cool shrug.

Afraid the illicit excitement swirling though her veins night be visible in her eyes, she evinced great interest in n invisible speck on her jeans before meeting his eyes. *Don't let him see what he's done to you, Nell,* she told erself. Smile pinned on, she looked up. Her heart sank… *Oh, God, he already knows!*

'Actually, I thought about what you said. Most of it was ubbish, but,' she admitted, 'I suppose you might have a oint when you said me being in the background like a bad mell is constantly reminding them of the past. Maybe it vould be better if I kept a low profile for a while.'

'I do not recall likening you to a bad smell.'

'You didn't have to.' She gave an indifferent smile to nderline that his opinion was of the utmost indifference to er. 'It's obvious what you think of me and I don't…'

'I like the way you…' The muscles in his sexily hollow

cheeks clenched as he swallowed. 'I have changed m
mind. I think you should remain a part of Katerina an
Antonio's life. They need you.'

His volte-face made her suspect the worst. 'Has some
thing happened?'

'Katerina did not come home last night, but that is no
the reason for my change of heart.' He watched her; a
expression of alarm spread across Nell's face.

'Is she all right?'

'Do not be alarmed. She is unharmed—for the moment.
he added darkly.

Nell gave a relieved sigh and eased her bottom onto th
edge of one of the tables. 'Driving you crazy, is she? I
doesn't sound like Kate, the staying-out-all-night thing. Ar
you sure there were no crossed wires?'

'Positive.'

'Maybe she forgot the time. Didn't you ring to find ou
what was happening?' she puzzled.

'We didn't know where she was,' he admitted bluntly
'I allowed her the freedom you suggested and this is th
result of the new tolerant regime.'

'Tolerant, not *stupid*!' Nell exclaimed. 'You can't jus
chuck the rule book out with the bath water,' she explaine
earnestly, mixing her clichés.

'This may come as a shock to you, Miss Rose, but peopl
are not in the habit of telling me I am stupid.'

'Believe me,' she breathed, 'it shows.'

There was a silence and then to her total amazement h
threw back his head and laughed. It was a warm, uninhib
ited and incredibly attractive sound.

His laughter died away but he continued to watch he
with a quizzical expression. 'I'm curious—do you think
would become a nicer, kinder, cuddlier, more politicall
correct person if I was insulted occasionally?'

The day anyone mentioned cuddly and Raul Carreras in the same breath was the day hungry wolves became old ladies' favourite lap-dogs.

'And deprive all your boot-lickers of job satisfaction?' She gave a disingenuous smile. 'I wouldn't be so cruel, but don't worry if you need your ego pricking—children are good at that.'

'So are you.' He didn't smile, but neither did he look annoyed. He looked...? Nell couldn't quite put her finger on it, but she knew the intensity he was radiating made her feel uneasy.

She shrugged. 'It's one of my only talents,' she explained, trying to introduce a note of lightness.

'What about your...was it painting or sculpture?' he queried.

'I painted.'

He was quick to pick up on her use of tense. 'But you don't now?'

'Oh, I'm not good enough to make a living out of it. Xavier made me see that.'

A frown forming on his lean features, Raul scanned her face with disapproval. 'And he was the expert?'

'Well, yes, he was.'

'You seem very untroubled about your loss of a dream,' he observed.

'What do you know about my dreams?' she charged, angered by his disapproving tone.

'I know I feature in them upon occasion.'

The sly observation made Nell catch her breath.

With an air of languid interest Raul watched the hot, guilty colour flood her pale face. 'The morning after the night I spent on your sofa?'

Nell gave a fractured sigh of relief. 'I thought you'd...' She stopped. Well, she could hardly tell him that he'd played a major role in all her dreams since and to her shame she wasn't always asleep! 'That was strictly a one-off.' Nell could hear the bluster in her own voice and hoped like hell he couldn't.

'You never know when your subconscious is going to hijack you, or so I've found,' he drawled.

Nell shot him a surprised look but found no evidence of the unusual note she had heard in his voice on his dark lean features.

'Don't you think that it is a defeatist attitude to give up on your dream?'

His preoccupation with the subject of her lack of talent was beginning to irritate. 'Determination is not a substitute for talent.' Accepting that she didn't have what it took had been one of the hardest things in her life. 'It's better to be realistic than waste a lot of time trying for something you'll never achieve. I don't want to be mediocre.'

His shrewd eyes searched her face. 'Is that a direct quote?' One dark brow arched.

Nell flushed. 'Nobody puts words in my mouth.'

Her angry claim brought his dark eyes zeroing in on her wide, soft lips. The brooding expression in them sent her stomach into a lurching nosedive.

'Don't you think the public should be allowed to make their own mind up about what constitutes art? Haven't many of the artists we now consider great been vilified by critics when they lived? If they had shown your spineless attitude the world would have been robbed of their legacy.'

Nell blinked at the vehemence in his quiet voice. 'I am not an original. I am a dabbler like thousands of others. The world didn't lose anything when I hung up my brushes.'

'You don't have to be an expert at something to get a lot of pleasure trying to do it better.'

The beginnings of a suspicion that they were no longer discussing art was just forming in her mind when Raul's next words confirmed it.

'I was pretty clueless at kissing once, but improving my technique provided me many hours of innocent pleasure.'

Nell ran the tip of her tongue along her dry lips, wanting, but unable, to tear her eyes from his dark face. *'Innocent?'*

Raul shrugged. 'Well, these things are relative,' he admitted huskily.

'You can hardly compare painting to kissing.'

'Both are an art form.'

'I suppose you consider yourself some sort of expert?'

The febrile glitter in his eyes spelt danger. 'Is that a challenge?'

She pressed a hand to her throat; she could feel the vibration of her pulse through her fingertips. 'Most definitely n...not.' Her attempt to sound firm and faintly amused by his response failed abysmally. 'I'm quite willing to accept you are the world's best kisser without a demonstration.' Her amused laughter faded away in the face of his unblinking, expressionless stare. 'You didn't come here to kiss me,' she protested.

A strange expression flickered into his dark eyes. 'Didn't I?' He gave a twisted smile, which faded to a look of deadly intent. 'Then if I didn't I should have.' The smile that formed on his lips nailed her feet to the floor. Her mind went blank as he advanced towards her. She just stood, her eyes wide, anticipation curling hot in the pit of her stomach.

Her face lifted to his even before he framed her face between his big hands. His jaw tightened, drawing the golden flesh tight over his incredible bone structure.

'Sexual attraction is a curious thing, is it not?' Lazily he skimmed the smooth surface of her cheek with the pad of his thumb. Nell closed her eyes tight. The contact made every nerve in her body quiver. In every individual cell she was aware and deeply excited by the virile strength of the man who stood beside her.

A sliver of savage satisfaction slid into Raul's eyes as he felt her slender body tremble.

She made a last-ditch attempt to break the spell he was weaving. 'This macho stuff leaves me cold,' she claimed shakily.

He slid a burnished strand through his fingers and watched it slither free. The sight seemed to fascinate him. 'I don't think so.' His deep, accented voice had a drugging, hypnotic quality.

He lowered his dark head until his face was on a level with hers. Holding her eyes, his traced the outline of her lips with the tip of his tongue. The compulsion to touch her own tongue to his was one she could no longer repress.

She felt a deep sigh shudder through his body as he wound his fingers into her hair, preventing her drawing back, only Nell felt no desire to pull back—she was hooked! Nothing in her life had prepared her for what she was feeling.

'This feels…'

'I know…' A throaty sound of encouragement vibrated in his throat as their breaths mingled. He pressed his lips to the corner of her mouth. The teasing butterfly caresses continued. If this tentative probing, the advance-and-retreat technique, was meant to leave her wanting more, it worked—oh, it *definitely* worked!

Nell's hands were balled into fists. She was shaking and her entire body convulsed with anticipation and longing by the time his tongue slid deeply between her parted lips. The searing kiss plunged her into a world of unimaginable delight; she responded with instincts she didn't know she possessed with a hunger that seemed a match for the rampant demands of his skilful lips.

When they broke apart, Raul, with his hands on her shoulders, pushed her a little way from him and looked into her passion-glazed eyes.

'Well, now I know.'

Nell blinked in a bemused fashion up at his fabulous face and wondered if he was going to do that again.

'Know what…?'

'I know what it feels like to kiss you. I know why Javier didn't mind people sniggering behind his back.'

Nell flinched as though he had struck her and stepped back. Raul's hand fell from her shoulders and he made no attempt to re-establish contact. So was that what it had been about—his curiosity, some nasty little experiment? Her chin went up. She would have died before she'd let him see how much he had hurt her.

'And now I know how you kiss and, let me tell you, it wasn't so very marvellous.'

'Perhaps I should employ you on a permanent basis? To deflate my ego,' he added.

She felt bereft and close to tears. 'I suspect the novelty of someone telling you when you're being impossibly arrogant would wear off pretty quickly,' she responded with a dry laugh.

'You consider me arrogant?'

'I consider you something else, Mr Carreras,' she replied, her body still shaken by intermittent tremors.

'I think we should be on a first-name basis now, don't you? Under the circumstances…'

'Now, as much as I'm enjoying this frank exchange of views, do you think we could get back to why you tracked me down here?'

'You are very businesslike.'

'No, but I am hungry.' Their eyes met and she flushed. *'For food,'* she snapped angrily. Actually, food was a pretty good idea; she had skipped lunch and had a sickening headache, which she knew from painful experience would get worse if she didn't eat something soon. 'It is late,' she reminded him, glancing pointedly at her watch. 'And you still haven't told me anything you couldn't have over the phone.'

'I could not have kissed you over the phone.'

'I knew there was a reason I liked telephones. Now, shall we get down to business?'

'Am I keeping you from a dinner date?'

'Dressed like this?' she responded, placing her hands on her slim, denim-covered hips. With a rueful smile on her lips, she looked up and found his eyes were fixed on the curves her actions had draw attention to. When the expression in those dark, glittering depths snuffed out her smile and sent her stomach muscles into spasm.

Time for a reality check—Raul had kissed her because she had dared to question his ability and he'd wanted to give her marks out of ten. He was like a male animal whose supremacy had been challenged. He was callous and shallow and she hated him.

The only problem was that her hate morphed into something far warmer when he touched her.

The kiss that had blown her mind had meant less than nothing to him. And that smouldering look was as much a reflex as a sneeze. Nell had learnt a long time ago that imagining women undressed was something your average male had about as much control over as sneezing. They were not wildly discriminating, you didn't have to be fantastically sexy, which made her overreacting to a look in this way plain daft.

'I have a microwave lasagne with my name on it.'

To Nell's intense relief her gentle prod brought his eyes back to her face.

'I have come to run an idea by you.'

She was so worried by her own heightened colour, it didn't occur to Nell that his own darker skin tones were significantly deeper than normal. 'Go ahead, then.'

'Would you agree that Alex and Katerina like you, they trust you…?'

Wondering where this was leading, Nell nodded warily. 'I think they do.'

'And you are fond of them?'

'Is that a trick question?' She closed her eyes and hissed in exasperation, 'Just cut to the chase.'

'As you wish.' He gave one of his inimical shrugs. 'I have a business proposition to put to you.'

'Oh?'

'I have heavy work commitments. My mother is not a young woman, her eyesight is failing and she is making herself ill trying to look after her grandchildren.'

'There must be some way to make her slow down.'

'There is. You move into our London house to ease the children through the transition they must make.'

CHAPTER SEVEN

'ME, MOVE into your house!' Nell exclaimed, her eyes widening in horror.

A significant proportion of her horror could be accounted for by the first, knee-jerk thought that popped into her head, namely—*What are the chances I will bump into him wearing a bath towel or something similar?*

Not only did this illustrate her growing unhealthy obsession with his body, it wasn't even realistic. The Carrerases almost certainly lived in the sort of mansion where you could go two days without seeing another human being.

Face hot with shame, she grunted. 'You must be joking.'

'No, I am reliably informed I have no sense of humour,' he explained, deadpan.

This drew a reluctant grin from Nell. 'Katerina?'

Raul nodded.

Nell gave a grimace of wry sympathy—about time she started putting the children's needs ahead of her own base instincts. Not that her concern for them was going to make her do anything as stupid as moving into the Carreras mansion.

'I can see things are hard for you at the moment, but they'll get better,' she promised him.

'I'm disappointed,' he admitted with an air of candour. 'I didn't think you were the sort of person whose caring stopped at the point where it inconvenienced you.'

Her eyes narrowed. 'You can cut out the moral blackmail right now.'

'You must admit I have a point. They do not need a

nanny, they need a friend, a familiar face in a strange place. You would not be there in an official capacity. You would simply be our guest.'

'I'm not going to admit anything, and for the record I'm not bothered about being inconvenienced, I'm bothered about…'

'Yes?' he prompted.

Her eyes slid from his. 'It's just a daft idea.'

'I'm not asking you to marry me.'

'Pity, they say laughter is good for you. On the other hand it's probably just as well,' she interrupted loudly. 'I doubt if your fiancée would like it.'

'*My fiancée?* I don't have a fiancée, so there is one obstacle removed.'

'I suppose you'll say next that Roxie Allan is just a good friend.'

'No, I'm just sleeping with her.'

His expression grew faintly amused as her lips moved in a faint moue of shocked distaste.

'Have I said something to offend you?'

Nell made a point of taking what she read in the tabloids with a pinch of salt, but this conversation went a long way to confirm the heartless womaniser image the media had consigned to him. His callous attitude to women horrified her.

'Does the lady in question know she's *just* sleeping with you?'

'Roxie?'

'You mean there are some others who are planning a spring wedding?'

'I suspect that Roxie's publicists are responsible for leaking most of those "exclusives".'

'And you don't care?' His casual attitude to having his

business, or a version of it at least, plastered over the tabloids perplexed her.

'The day I do decide to get married the newspapers will *not* be the first people to know, and, incidentally, I have never had to promise marriage to a woman to get her into bed.'

His assurance set her teeth on edge.

'But then you've never tried it without the seductiveness of the Carreras millions behind you.'

Even as she made the sly suggestion, Nell was privately acknowledging that even if Raul had not had a penny to his name he would still have had women falling over themselves to catch his attention.

What Raul had money couldn't buy.

'No, but Javier did.'

'*You're* not Javier.'

A flinty gleam entered his eyes in response to her angry taunt. 'Why do you need to flaunt the fact you were my brother's mistress every two seconds?' Anger emanated from every inch of his rigid, disapproving frame.

Nell shook her head; even by his standards this hypocrisy was breathtaking. 'You're the one who introduced Javier into the conversation,' she reminded him. 'And I don't recall saying I was his mistress.'

The muscles of his strong brown throat worked as he regarded her with extreme distaste. 'No, you just happened to live in the same house as him for two years. How dare you look down your little nose at someone like Roxie?'

The insult stung. 'I was looking down my nose at you, not her!'

His expressive lips formed the definitive sneer. 'Are you trying to tell me you didn't sleep with my brother?'

'What would be the point?' she demanded sarcastically.

'A man and a woman can't have a relationship that doesn't include sex, can they?'

Eyes dark as night swept over her face. 'Not if one of them is Spanish.'

The throaty observation sent a secret shiver of excitement shuddering through her hopelessly receptive body. 'Spaniards didn't invent sex, you know,' she said through gritted teeth.

'No, we merely perfected it. You have personal experience—Javier, even without his *seductive Carreras millions*, still managed to lure one of the most beautiful women I've ever seen into his bed.'

'Did you know Cathy?' she began, an eager note entering her voice. She had seen photos of the wife Javier had adored and had thought her very lovely. 'Kate looks very like her, don't you think?'

'No doubt.' His interest in family resemblance seemed minimal. 'However, I wasn't talking about Cathy.'

'Then who—?' She stopped, her eyes widening to their full extent when his meaning sank in. Her body went through a series of extreme temperature variations before settling to an all-over tingling glow.

'Save the tired old chat-up lines for someone who appreciates them, please.' Nell tried to sound bored and not breathless, though she didn't know why she bothered to keep up the pretence. It was far too much like locking the stable door after the proverbial horse had bolted. Raul was far too experienced not to pick up on what she was feeling; besides, she had responded to his kiss with all the subtlety of a sex-starved bimbo!

Raul studied her flushed cheeks with interest. 'Does me finding you attractive make you nervous?'

And wouldn't you like that? she thought grimly. Actually, him finding her attractive was something she didn't—

couldn't—deal with. Her adolescence had not involved being a victim to her hormones in a problematic way and she was not enjoying the experience now it had caught up with her. Caught up with a vengeance!

'I won't even dignify that with an answer,' she returned loftily. Then almost immediately contradicted herself by adding, 'Actually, it makes me nauseous.'

Raul, obviously not a man with a self-esteem problem, laughed.

'Well, if I ever had any doubts about taking you up on your so kind offer—*I don't now*!' she declared coldly. 'Sleep in the same bed as you?' She winced to hear her voice rise to an unattractive, scathing squeak.

One dark brow lifted to a satirical angle. *'Bed?'*

'What?' she snapped, with an impatient frown.

'Bed. You said "sleep in the same bed as you."'

Nell went hot, cold and then hot again. 'I did not!' *Did I?* 'I said under the same roof.'

'Freudian slip?' he suggested. 'Or wishful thinking?'

Her face flamed. 'You really do think a lot of yourself, don't you?' she choked.

'You don't find confidence an attractive trait in a man? Most women do.'

'That's what they say to your face.'

Her hissing retort made him grin. It was perverse that when she actually *tried* to make him mad he acted as if it were some big joke, and yet when she said something perfectly innocent he acted as if he wanted to throttle her.

Definitely perverse!

'You mean they are willing to overlook my character defects because of my wealth?' A hard edge crept into his languid tone as his deep-set eyes swept over her heated face. 'Was it Javier's name that drew you to him?'

The interrogative note that had entered his voice made her frown.

'Did you move on when you discovered he had the name, but not the money?' he persisted.

'It would hardly have taken me two years to discover he had no money, and, as for leaving him, I didn't. He chucked me out.' She had been reluctant to leave the security and set up alone, but Javier had been firm. It had been time she'd moved on; being with him had been stopping her forming new relationships; she'd needed to spread her wings, he had said.

Nell had stopped resisting when she had realised that this had applied equally to himself. Her presence might have made it difficult for Javier to form new relationships and perhaps he'd been feeling ready to do so.

For a moment Raul looked totally disconcerted by her response. 'I don't believe it!'

'That's sweet of you, but not everyone finds me as irresistible as you. Even the most warm and appealing of us have our faults, though you probably don't hang around long enough to find out about your girlfriends' irritating habits,' she added drily. 'Do you ever see them without their make-up?'

'Are you trying to tell me my brother seduced a girl young enough to be his…?' Raul broke off, closed his eyes and inhaled. His struggle for control was written visibly on his taut, strong-boned features. 'My brother would not seduce a teenager and then discard her when the novelty had worn off.'

The penny finally dropped.

A look of comprehension spread across Nell's face. Raul needed to see her as a scheming hussy because the alternative made his brother, the brother she was beginning to realise that he had idolised, the sleazy sort of guy who targeted young, inexperienced girls. It was so blindingly simple she didn't know why it hadn't occurred to her earlier. The more she considered the theory, the more sense it made. It certainly explained his hostility.

'Javier did not seduce me,' she said quietly.

'It is unnecessary for you to tell me this.'

'And,' she continued firmly, 'I did not seduce him. It wasn't about anyone being used. We just needed one another.' Raul received this information with a stony expression.

'You do not need to draw a picture for me.' The pictures Raul was seeing in his head were altogether graphic enough. 'I do not need a lesson in *needing*.'

Nell's blue eyes sparkled with anger. 'You always have to sink everything to the lowest common denominator, don't you? I'm not talking about sex.'

'So you consider sex the "lowest common denominator"?'

Nell flushed and looked away from his mocking eyes. 'There are other things. Things that are equally important. I...I cooked and cleaned.'

'You cooked and cleaned?' he echoed.

'Yes,' she agreed, warming to her theme. 'And looked after the children.'

'You are trying to tell me you were some sort of au pair?'

'No, it wasn't a formal arrangement.'

'Very much like the one I am suggesting, then.'

'Nothing like.'

The dark lashes dipped over his eyes before slowly lifting. He angled his head so that their glances sealed. The sharp contours of his carved cheekbones were accentuated by two bands of dull colour. Nell could see the silver flecks deep in his eyes; they had a hypnotic quality.

A shiver rippled through her body. Painfully conscious

of the heat low in her belly, she tried to swallow, only couldn't. Her throat muscles seemed to be paralysed. She pulled nervously at the neck of her sweater; she wanted to look away but couldn't.

Couldn't or didn't want to…?

'It could be?' Sinfully soft, seductively suggestive, his words hung in the air between them.

Raul was under the impression her arrangement with Javier had reached the bedroom. She released the breath she had been unconsciously holding in a fractured gasp as her brain made the necessary connections.

'I don't even like you.' She had never been tempted by casual sex…*but would it be such a terrible thing?* Shocked by the direction of her thoughts, she took a deep breath. 'And you don't like me.'

His mobile mouth twisted in a cynical smile as he shrugged. 'Does that matter?'

Nell stared at him, seeing only his careless attitude and not the tension that held his lean body taut. Her anger stirred. 'To me it does.'

'You're not going to deny that things happen whenever we are in the same room?'

She didn't deny or confirm his observation. 'When I sleep with a man it won't be someone who looks on the experience as no more important than ordering a meal or choosing a bottle of wine.'

'I drink very little, and I leave what I eat to my chef. Sex is something I give a great deal more thought to and I am not considered a selfish lover.'

The physical craving when she looked at him was almost a physical pain. 'I'm not looking for a lover!' she blurted before she could say or do something that would reveal how sorely she was tempted.

To her total chagrin he took her rejection of his advances

pretty calmly. With a philosophical shrug, to be precise. Nell had seen people get more emotional about missing a bus!

'But you will be looking for a job, apparently.'

'It looks like it,' she said through gritted teeth.

'And I don't suppose your landlord will be prepared to wait for the rent? But I expect you have savings put aside for such a rainy day.'

Nell, who hadn't yet had time to seriously consider the practical aspects of being unemployed, regarded his classic profile with simmering dislike. 'Of course,' she lied airily.

'I didn't think so.'

'All right,' she flared. 'I don't, but, before you get excited about the idea of me being thrown out onto the street, I should explain that working here isn't my only source of income.'

'Oh?'

'I work the late shift in a convenience store three nights a week. They'll be more than happy to extend my hours.'

'A convenience store?' he repeated, looking at her as though she had just disembarked from a spaceship.

'Yes, a convenience store, and I have had an offer to be a life model at the art school. It pays good money. I have a couple of friends who did it when we were at college.'

The muscles in his brown throat worked. 'You would take off your clothes in front of strangers?' Raul was conscious of the dull roar in his head building in volume as his imagination provided a picture of a bunch of drooling, lascivious men lusting over Nell's naked body.

Nell gave a disdainful little sniff. 'There's nothing smutty about it,' she flared defensively. 'The human body is a perfectly natural, beautiful thing.'

A muscle clenched in Raul's cheek. 'Some more beautiful than others.' The studied insolence of his bold survey brought Nell's arms up in an instinctively protective gesture.

'Do you really think you have what it takes to be an artist's model?'

Nell's arms fell away; she was unsure whether this comment referred to her body or her modesty. She could have told him that she was only self-conscious about her body when he was around.

'Modelling is art,' she contended.

'Oh, well that makes it all right, then,' Raul drawled with acid sarcasm that brought an angry glitter to her eyes. 'And how can you be so sure that all the people who come to draw naked women are inspired to do so by such pure and elevated motives as you ascribe to them?' he demanded. 'Do you not think it conceivable that some actually come to ogle nubile young women who they would not normally get within five feet of?'

'Just because you have a disgusting mind, don't assume that everyone else has.'

Raul released a dry laugh. 'I find if you assign the worst possible motives to people you are rarely disappointed.'

'Which means you wouldn't recognise someone who was actually on the level,' she cried, appalled by his cynicism.

He gave a thin-lipped smile. 'I'll take that chance.'

'And I,' she retorted, 'will take off my clothes if I wish, despite narrow-minded bigots like you!'

'I would pay you more not to.'

This driven, extraordinary statement took the wind out of her sails. 'You would do *what*?'

A self-conscious expression slid across his face before his extravagant lashes came down, brushing the slashing contours of his bold cheekbones before lifting.

'I mean that living in my home would solve your finan-

cial problems and my domestic ones. Unless taking off you
clothes in public is the culmination of a lifelong ambition?'

Before Nell had chance to respond to this outrageou
suggestion he took her elbow and led her towards the door
'You should never make a decision on an empty stomach
Let me buy you dinner. Your bag?' he asked, picking up
her leather satchel.

Shocked into temporary submission by his hands-on ap
proach to taking charge of the situation, Nell nodded.

'Coat?'

She shook her head.

Raul clicked off the light switch. 'Aren't you forgettin
something?' he asked, looking down at her as they steppe
out into the night.

Nell shivered as the cold night air penetrated her sweater
When she had dressed that morning it had been a fine au
tumn morning, but it had been raining for the better par
of the day and the street lights were reflected in the rain
soaked pavements.

'That I have a will of my own?' She wouldn't min
betting that a lot of women did that around Raul.

He grinned mechanically at her self-condemnatory quip
and inclined his head towards the door, which stood open

'Oh, I forgot,' she said, flustered as she reached for th
keys on her belt. Aware in just about every cell of her bod
of the man watching her, she clumsily inserted the key int
the lock and turned it.

She brushed the hair from her eyes and attempted t
regain control of the situation, show him that he couldn'
push her around.

'I'll eat with you if you promise not to mention me mov
ing in. That's the deal, take it or leave it,' she explained.

'I'll take it.' He held open the passenger door of the low
slung saloon.

Nonplussed by his easy capitulation, she stared at first the car and secondly the driver. 'But I thought...'

A smile of worrying complacency spread across his impossibly perfect features. 'Then you thought wrong. And not for the first time,' he added enigmatically under his breath. 'Just get in.'

'I'm not dressed for...'

'Reneging on a deal, Nell?'

Nell cast him a look of acute dislike and slid into the low-slung car.

CHAPTER EIGHT

NOT only did Raul not introduce the taboo subject of Nell
moving in during the journey, he didn't introduce any subject. He didn't actually say anything until he had parked
the car.

'We're here.'

'Where?' she asked, getting out of the car.

Raul pointed at the grand-looking Georgian terrace they
had drawn up in front of.

'Is this a hotel? Because I can tell you now a place like
that won't serve me dressed like this.'

Raul mounted the steps that swept up to a porticoed entrance and gestured her to follow him. 'It's not a hotel.'

Frowning at his evasive response, she did reluctantly follow him. The door opened before they reached it. A man
in uniform stood there. Nell had a very bad feeling about
this.

'Is my mother still up, James?'

'Yes, sir,' the impassive flunky replied. 'She is in the
kitchen.'

God, was I slow not to see this one coming, Nell chas-
tised herself.

'I'm not going in there.'

Raul spun back to her, his preoccupied expression suggesting he'd forgotten she existed.

'I want to go home,' she wailed.

'Dios mìo!' With an expression of exasperation he
caught her hand and virtually frogmarched her into the

84

house. A house that just happened to have an entrance hall you could have fitted a football pitch in.

Blinking at the brightness of the illumination provided by umpteen chandeliers suspended from a ceiling covered with elaborate mouldings, she snatched her hand from his and rounded on him furiously.

'This is kidnap,' she claimed wildly. 'I'll report you to the police!'

Raul did not look unduly put out by the threat and the impassive manservant focused on some point above her head and excused himself. Clearly as far as he was concerned his employer was at liberty to kidnap as many women as he chose to.

'I think you're overreacting slightly,' Raul commented mildly. 'However, after we eat you can report me to whoever you please, and ask for Chief Superintendent Pritchard. He's a good man—mention my name.'

'You think that just because you're rich you can do anything you like!' she accused loudly. 'You planned this,' she added in a throbbing undertone.

His laid his hand lightly across her forehead.

Her reaction to his touch was instantaneous and intense; her temperature shot up several degrees and her stomach dissolved.

'Ah, I diagnose a blood-sugar dip and a tendency to dramatise.'

Complicated by lust. Nell regained enough control to pull back. Panting gently, she angrily tugged her feathery fringe back down to cover the area he had just touched.

'I prescribe a traditional supper of paella.'

'I suppose you have a team of flunkies waiting to cook anything you fancy at any time of the day or night.'

'No, my mother is in the kitchen. My mother does not believe in therapy, but when she is stressed she cooks. She can only cook one dish, but,' he added, looking into Nell's confused face, 'she cooks it very well.'

Nell attributed his comments to a bizarre sense of humour until they actually entered the kitchen, a vast, cavernous room on the lower-ground-floor level, which, it seemed to an envious Nell, incorporated every modern appliance known to man.

These gleaming appliances and the sleek units that housed them sat cheek by jowl with impressive period features such as a lead-blackened range, original bread oven and flagstone floors. The combination could have looked odd, but the stainless steel modernity married happily with the traditional.

'This is Nell.'

Nell stepped forward. She didn't actually have much choice in the matter; there was a firm hand in the small of her back propelling her in that direction. She slung a resentful scowl over her shoulder before arranging her features into an expression of polite neutrality.

The woman standing stirring a saucepan on the stainless steel hob looked from Raul to Nell. The genuine smile of delight that revealed laughter lines around her glittering eyes made it hard not to smile back. Maybe some people might be able to resist such charm and warmth, but Nell was not one of them.

'I know who this is. I am Aria Carreras.' The woman who identified herself as Raul's mother possessed an attractive husky voice made huskier by the emotion in it. 'I am so glad you came!' she cried as she floated toward Nell with the sort of natural grace that many a dancer would have envied.

Several inches taller than Nell and slim as a wand, she stooped forward and enclosed Nell in a fragrant hug, then rawing back, she kissed the startled younger woman oundly on both cheeks.

'You were expecting me?'

'Of course we were, and so pretty, Raul!' she exclaimed, unning a knuckle of her beautifully manicured hand softly own the curve of an astonished Nell's cheek. Then as she urned to her son an indignant expression spread across her ne-boned patrician features. 'Why didn't you tell me she vas so pretty?' she scolded, wagging her finger at him.

Because his taste runs to obvious blondes with legs that o on forever and gravity-defying bosoms, Nell thought, eriving a small degree of satisfaction from the flash of atent discomfiture that chased across his dark, devastatngly gorgeous features as he took the brunt of his parent's easing censure.

'And don't tell me you didn't notice, Raul.'

'I've noticed.'

Nell's lowered gaze lifted, and was instantly snared by is bold, glittering stare. Transfixed by the combination of exual challenge and hunger in his half-closed eyes, she ought a crazy compulsion to walk straight into his arms.

The craziness didn't stop there. She had no more control ver the breath she felt escape her parted lips in a long, emulous sigh than she did the pulse of sexual longing that tabbed through her. There was a whooshing sound like the ea in her ears as she stood there feeling the vibration of ach individual thud of her heartbeat echo like a drumbeat n her throat. She struggled to catch her breath and shake erself free of an atmosphere that literally crackled with exual tension.

'I feel I already know you; the children speak of you all he time.'

Nell heard the older woman's words as if they came from great distance away. She made an enormous effort and

dragged her attention back to her. She gave a vague, dis
orientated smile and cleared her throat.

'I really didn't have any idea they meant to run away
she promised the older woman earnestly.

'Why, we never imagined you did, my dear. Did we
Raul?'

'No, I suppose you would have to be a particularly para
noid and suspicious person to think that,' Nell cut i
sweetly.

'And you were a friend to my dear Javier when h
needed a friend.' Her liquid dark eyes filled. 'For that w
shall always be in your debt.'

Nell, who had assumed that the entire Carreras famil
would share Raul's view of her relationship with Javie
made some self-deprecating, embarrassed gesture. He
thoughts were in a whirl.

'Won't we, Raul?'

Nell held her breath.

'Eternally.'

Nell released her breath. His mother seemed oblivious t
the ironic quality in his response that made her own cheek
burn angrily.

And Raul's mother? Nell was finding it extremely har
to reconcile this svelte youthful figure, who oozed vitalit
and exuded the sort of effortless style that so many wome
tried fruitlessly all their lives to achieve, with her ment
image of a bedridden little old lady with failing eyesight

Her outraged gaze swivelled again towards the man wh
had provided her with this erroneous image. He smiled la
guidly back at her, not a trace of embarrassment or discon
fort in his manner. The man, she decided in disgus
wouldn't recognise a scruple if he fell over it! Were the
no depths to which he would not sink, no web of lies h
would not spin in order to get his own way?

Pretty pointless too, considering she was obviously going to find out that his mother was hardly the candidate for a nursing home.

'Raul said that you would come.' Aria smiled at her son, revealing lines around her beautiful almond-shaped eyes. 'You have no idea at all how relieved this makes me.'

It dawned on a dismayed Nell that Raul's mother believed that she had come to stay. Had that been Raul's intention? Of course it had. Well, if he was relying on her being too embarrassed to correct this false impression—one he had obviously cynically cultivated—he was going to be disappointed.

She was so furious with him she didn't trust herself to look at him. *Is anger the only reason you're scared to look at him?* the cynical voice in her head enquired drily.

'Actually I just came for supper.'

'Of course you did.' The older woman patted her arm and drew her towards the table. 'Do have a seat—you look tired.'

'I think there's been some misunderstanding,' Nell began uncomfortably as she took a chair at the long refectory table. 'I've not *come*, that is, I've not come to stay.'

'You haven't?' The mature and beautiful brunette turned a look of questioning appeal in her son's direction.

'We are still negotiating terms.' Nell was frustrated to hear him make it sound like a done deal. 'But I have no doubt that the outcome will be one that is beneficial to us all.'

Not if I have anything to say about it, Nell thought as she listened to his deliberately ambiguous words.

'You must not let him bully you. My son always thinks he knows what is best for other people.'

'You mean he thinks he's always right?' Nell nodded and sent Raul a spitefully sweet smile. 'Yes, I'd noticed that, actually it's hard to miss, but don't worry, I won't,' Nell promised.

The older woman looked at her with amusement. 'I believe you,' she decided, sounding pleased by this discovery. 'Turn that hob down for me, Raul!' she instructed without looking at her son.

'It's not on.'

'I did turn it off by mistake, but I distinctly recall turning it back on.'

'The back burner is on,' Raul inserted gently.

A spasm of distress, which seemed to Nell disproportionate to the mild domestic blip, contorted the classical features of the older woman as she sat down heavily in a chair.

'I do that sort of thing all the time,' said Nell.

'It's not the same. These wretched eyes,' Aria cried, passing a hand across the items she had cursed. Her expression was tinged with embarrassment as she turned to Nell. 'I expect Raul has mentioned that my eyesight is not as good as it might be?'

'He did,' she confessed uncomfortably. 'But I thought…' Nell stopped mid-sentence; you could hardly tell a fond mother that you had thought her son was a liar who had invented a sick parent.

'What did you think, my dear?'

Her cheeks burning, Nell's eyes automatically sought out the tall, silent figure who had left the stove and was crossing the room. Their eyes locked and his knowing expression confirmed her worst fears—he was perfectly aware that she had assumed he'd been lying about his mother's condition.

'I expect you thought that he was an over-anxious son exaggerating.' Unwittingly it was Aria who came to her rescue. 'I only wish he was,' she admitted with a sigh.

Before Nell could respond to this wistful comment Raul came to stand behind his mother. He laid a hand on her shoulder and said something soft and rapid in Spanish. Whatever he said drove the melancholy expression from her face and drew forth her light, musical laughter.

'Mother has diabetes. It went undiagnosed for some time and unfortunately it has affected her eyesight.'

'Yes, I have diabetic retinopathy. The doctors are hopeful that the damage has been arrested, however I am still adjusting. An adjustment, which, as Raul rightly says, would be a lot easier if I wasn't so vain. They want me to use a white stick. *A white stick!*' she exclaimed with an eloquent shudder before sliding seamlessly into her native tongue.

Nell's expression grew thoughtful as she listened to the to and fro of conversation between mother and son. 'Does it need to be white?'

The conversation stopped.

'I was just wondering, if the idea is for you to be able to feel obstructions, the colour of the stick really doesn't matter, does it?'

'I really don't see what relevance the colour is.'

Refusing to be put off by Raul's dismissive manner, Nell persisted. 'I mean, people have handbags to match their outfits—why not canes? You could start a new fashion.' She shrugged as silence greeted her comment. 'It was just a thought.'

'And a particularly foolish one.'

Nell's chin went up to a belligerent angle. 'I was only trying to be helpful; there's no need to be rude.' She watched his expression darken with annoyance. 'Would it be foolish if *you* had thought of it?'

'I wouldn't have because I—'

'Because you are a man,' his mother interceded. Nell's

moment of triumph was short-lived. 'It will be so nice to have another woman around the place for a while.'

'Well, actually, I—'

Raul cut in with a frown. 'I thought you were going back home to Spain to rest when Nell moved in.'

Nell isn't going to move in! It was a simple enough thing to say, so why, oh, why couldn't she just say it? The longer she delayed, the harder it was going to be. Why hadn't Raul's mother turned out to be a horrid, cold aristocrat and not warm, genuine and very obviously in need of support?

'And I shall, only Nell and the children shall come with me.' She gave a pleased smile that invited their admiration. 'I really don't know why I hadn't thought of it earlier.'

'The children have school.'

His mother dismissed the educational needs argument with a shrug of her narrow shoulders. Despite herself Nell felt her lips twitch; she was beginning to see where Raul had inherited his single-minded—some might say pig-headed—focus from.

'Antonio and Katerina are both bright; they'll soon catch up on a little work. A few weeks away from this appalling weather will do us all good, and it will get Katerina away from those undesirable elements you are concerned about. Though I must say I think you're just making them more attractive by banning her seeing them. What do you think, Nell? It can't be so very long ago that you were that age yourself.'

'Forbidden fruit can often seem attractive.'

As she spoke Nell found her eyes irresistibly drawn to the stern but sensual line of Raul's incredible mouth. Perhaps if she stopped denying herself that particular forbidden fruit it would lose its appeal. Since in the first place she wasn't about to test the theory and secondly it could equally prove addictive, this conjecture was both pointless and dangerous.

'That's exactly what I said to Raul,' Aria agreed.

'I explain something to Antonio and he does not challenge me.' A perplexed frown knitted Raul's wide brow. 'You cannot be reasonable with the girl; she is totally irrational!' he complained.

'She is a teenage girl, Raul,' Nell reminded him, unable to keep the quiver of amusement from her voice. 'They are not,' she added gravely, 'renowned for their reasonableness.'

'And actually you weren't so reasonable this morning yourself. He forbade her to leave the house until she had changed her skirt,' Aria explained in a conspiratorial aside to Nell.

'Putting aside the fact she would have suffered hypothermia,' Raul inserted drily. 'Self-expression is one thing, wearing inappropriate and provocative clothes is another. It is a matter of common sense,' he decreed.

'Or prudery?' Nell suggested innocently.

His rock-like jaw tightened. 'Perhaps you would not think it so funny if you knew as I do what an adolescent boy thinks of every waking moment of the day.' He drew a hand roughly through his dark hair. His working week had involved saving a deal that could have cost millions and it had been as a walk in the park compared to being responsible for the moral and physical well-being of a teenage girl!

His mother gave a cajoling smile. 'Wouldn't you like a nice holiday in the sun with us? You look tired. Doesn't he, Nell?'

He looks fabulous!

'I cannot take a holiday, you know that, and neither can the children.'

'Have you ever been to Spain, Nell?'

Raul gave a grunt of sheer exasperation. Nell could see why; Aria was obviously not the type to drop an idea without a fight.

Nell threw Raul an agonised look. If he didn't throw her a lifeline she was going to have to disappoint this nice woman and that was something Nell didn't want to do. 'No, I haven't,' she admitted. 'Actually, I've never been out of the country at all.'

'Never?'

Aria Carreras looked as startled as someone who treated international travel as casually as she treated catching a bus—*except I don't have my own personal bus,* Nell thought wryly...

'Well, money was a bit tight when I was a kid.'

'You have a big family?'

Nell shook her head, aware that Raul was listening, no doubt sifting the information to see if there was any little detail he could use to manipulate her.

'I was an only child.'

'And I'm sure your parents are very proud of you.'

'They died just when I was in my first year at art college,' Nell, left with little choice, explained with the same quiet composure that had made people comment at the time of the accident 'how well Nell was coping.' Inside Nell hadn't been coping at all, but her tears had been kept for when she was alone.

Aria Carreras was not similarly inhibited when it came to showing emotion in public. Nell watched as her lovely eyes filled with tears.

'Then you're all alone!' she exclaimed.

'I have lots of good friends,' Nell, who instinctively shied away from pity, assured the older woman brightly.

'But friends aren't the same as family, are they, Raul?'

'No,' he agreed blandly. 'You can walk away from them.'

His mother laughed. 'Take no notice of him, Nell. Raul has a very strong sense of family. When his father became ill he put aside his own ambitions to run the family businesses and since his death he has been a rock.'

There was curiosity in Nell's eyes as she turned her head to look at the tall figure with the proud, arrogant profile. Her smooth brow puckered. It had never occurred to her that he had ever wanted anything but what he had—*power*, and lots of it. He seemed so comfortable with it, was it actually possible he had ever had other ambitions?

'Of course, if Javier had stayed the burden would not have been so immense.' His mother sighed sadly. 'But that was not to be. He and your father were so alike, that was the problem, Raul. Neither would give an inch.'

Her comment raised a possibility that Nell had previously not considered. Did Raul resent the brother who had left him alone to carry the mantle of power? Or was he glad to be the only heir to the crown with his elder brother gone?

'Did you lose your husband a long time ago?' she asked quietly.

The older woman looked startled. 'He died the day after Javier; I thought you knew.'

Nell caught her breath. 'I'm so awfully sorry, I didn't realise.' The poor woman. Nell could not begin to imagine how terrible it must have been to bury your son and husband within days of one another. Raul's protective attitude to his mother was perfectly understandable under the circumstances.

'I don't suppose there is any reason you should. Unlike with Javier, it was not a shock.' She gave a tremulous little sigh. 'Apparently there is frequently no warning for people suffering from Javier's heart condition, so tragic the victims are often even younger than he was...'

'So I understand.' Nell looked up and found Raul's eyes on her face. The intensity of his regard was unnerving.

'With my husband,' his widow continued sadly, 'it was quite different; we had been expecting it for some time. Eduardo could have lived for many more years, Nell,' she revealed, 'if he had made a few minor adjustments to his life, but that wasn't his way. He lived life on his terms.' She sighed. 'I had to accept that.'

'My father,' Raul explained in a grim manner that suggested he did *not* share his mother's philosophical attitude on the subject, 'was a pigheaded, selfish idiot, who never made an *adjustment* in his life.'

Aria laid a hand on her son's arm. 'Exactly,' she said quietly. 'So you are in no way to blame; the doctors said so.'

Nell saw some indefinable but strong emotion flare in Raul's eyes before he gently removed his mother's hand.

'I know. The heart attack could have occurred at any moment, but the fact remains that I told my father his son had died and that he was a stubborn old fool, and he promptly suffered a massive and fatal heart attack. If I had not been so brutal...?' His broad shoulders lifted.

Nell looked at his grim, strong face and knew that that was a question that would hang over his head for the rest of his life. It was so massively unfair! She felt a wave of tenderness that was frightening in its depth and intensity.

'Well, that's a ridiculous attitude to have!' She coloured uncomfortably as her impetuous exclamation turned her into the focus of attention.

'Nell frequently finds me ridiculous,' Raul explained drily to his mother. He turned back to Nell, his expression sardonic. 'I am as always indebted for your input,' he added politely, at his driest.

Nell's eyes flared. The defiant gesture brought a glimmer of admiration to Raul's eyes.

'Actually, when you come right down to it,' she mused, 'all that hair-shirt stuff is actually pretty self-indulgent. Well, I think it is, anyhow.'

'And you are right.'

Nell didn't hear Aria's warm intervention as a sudden aspect of this situation occurred to her. She hardly dared seek confirmation of her suspicions.

'Javier's condition…' Her eyes darted fearfully to Raul's face; a furrow appeared between his brows as he read the total panic in her darkened eyes. 'I read up on it on the net after…' she began in a flat monotone. She swallowed as her throat closed over and ran her tongue over her dry lips 'It c…can run in families…?' The icy fear that gripped her was physical in its intensity.

Her eyes moved back to Raul so vital, so alive… imagining there could be a silent killer—wasn't that how the medical text had described it?—waiting to steal his life? It was something she could not bring herself to contemplate.

Aria nodded. 'Yes, that's right.'

'There must be something!' Nell blurted out. 'I mean, medical science…'

'My dear child,' Aria cried in a horrified voice. 'I insisted after the doctors explained the situation that Raul and Javier's children have all the tests. The children got the all-clear. And so did you, didn't you, Raul?'

Nell blinked. 'Then he's not going to…' The lean face before her suddenly blurred and the distant roar in her ears got louder.

CHAPTER NINE

'TAKE some deep breaths.'

Nell, with her head pressed between her knees, did as the rough voice instructed. When she struggled against the hand on the back of her neck it immediately lifted. She smoothed back her hair as she straightened up, deeply mortified at making such a spectacle of herself.

How on earth was she going to explain away her dramatic overreaction to them when she couldn't explain it to herself?

'Sorry about that, I...'

'There is no need to apologise. I remember how I felt when I realised there was a possibility I would lose both my sons,' Aria recalled with a shudder.

But you're his mother, Nell felt like saying, *you're meant to feel like that. I, on the other hand, have no excuse. I am nothing to Raul and he is nothing to me...*

'It's the end of a pretty stressful day.' Even to her own ears this sounded pretty lame. 'And I lost my job.' She finally worked up the courage to look at Raul and discovered his piercing stare was every bit as suspicious as she had feared.

'How awful for you, but Raul has a great many people working for him—I'm sure he could find a place for someone as obviously talented as you are if you don't want to move in here.' She regarded her son with confident anticipation.

'No, I couldn't,' Raul responded, not bothering to sugar-coat his refusal. 'In fact the idea is frankly appalling,' he declared bluntly.

An angry spark appeared in Nell's eyes. 'Well, there's no need to be rude, and just for the record I wouldn't work for you if you paid me!'

'I won't be.'

'Actually,' Aria mused, her gentle voice cutting through the heated exchange, 'you could be right. Working with someone you are close to is often very difficult. I should know, I started out as your father's secretary.'

'But we're not close!' Nell protested uneasily.

'If you say so,' Aria agreed with a worrying knowing twinkle in her eyes. 'You know, I'm feeling rather tired. I just might go to bed; you know, I think I might sleep now,' she confided, pressing a maternal kiss on her son's lean cheek. 'Now don't get up. You two enjoy your supper.'

Nell, an expression of dawning dismay in her eyes, watched the elegant figure remove herself. 'She doesn't think we're...? *Does she?*'

'My mother is a hopeless romantic and more than capable of tuning out the real world when it suits her. It would seem it suits her to think you and I are romantically linked.'

'This is all your fault!' Nell wailed, turning reproachful eyes on his amused face—it did her ego no end of good to know he found the idea of them being romantically involved a joke. Obviously the only place Raul wanted to get intimate was in the bedroom!

'And you figure that out how, exactly?'

'You brought me here,' she said through gritted teeth.

'And you gave that extraordinary performance of concern at the thought of my imminent demise.'

Nell looked at him in miserable stricken silence, then he laughed. In the blink of an eye Nell's embarrassed unease transformed into white-hot wrath. *Nothing* could justify making a joke of such a subject.

'It wasn't a performance!' she yelled.

'I'm touched,' he contended unconvincingly in a tone that set Nell's teeth on edge. She scanned his handsome face with a look of loathing.

'I was concerned for your mother,' she spelt out, having almost convinced herself by this point that what she was saying was true. Well, she couldn't *really* care about such a cold, sarcastic rat, could she? 'She's a lovely person who has been through enough. As far as I'm concerned there are several million people I'd shed a tear over before you. In fact I wouldn't care if you dropped dead at my feet!' her reckless tongue led her to tastelessly and untruthfully declare.

'In that case you'll be pleased to know that I...'

Nell saw Raul's chin whip upwards as a guarded expression stole across his face.

'What will I be pleased to know?' Her astonished gaze identified the streaks of darker colour across the crest of his high cheekbones, which on anybody else she would have had no hesitation in identifying as a blush.

'Nothing.'

A sudden unbelievable explanation for his odd behaviour presented itself—so odd and off the wall that she instantly dismissed it. Then as she scanned his face with more closely she gave a gasp.

'Oh, my God!' she croaked, looking at him with horrified disbelief. 'You didn't take them, did you? You didn't take the tests after Javier died. You lied to your mother,' she accused hoarsely.

His lean features settled into an expression of chilly hauteur. 'What I did or did not do is none of your concern.'

This declaration tantamount to an admission drew a

strained laugh from her pale lips. 'How could you be so stupid?' she demanded. 'You expect me to pretend I don't know!' she cried hoarsely.

'You know nothing.'

She found his air of detachment totally mystifying. 'Don't you *want* to know?' If it were her, Nell was sure she would.

Raul, his expression one of seething frustration, flung up his hands in an expressive gesture. 'If I knew, what difference would it make? Tell me that.' Her silence lengthened and he gave vent to a dry laugh.

'Well…well, you could be careful.'

'Careful…? Madre mìa!' Eyes as hot as coal raked her face. 'You mean I could stop doing half the things that make my life worth living! I could sit around and wait to drop dead and break out in a cold sweat every time I imagine I feel a twinge. I will not let this thing rule my life.'

'Listen, Raul, you can't bury your head in the sand. There might be nothing wrong with you.'

'In which case tests are irrelevant.'

His skewed logic made her stare. How could an intelligent man talk this way? 'Except for peace of mind,' she suggested.

'My mind is perfectly peaceful,' he ground out from between clenched white teeth.

'What about when you marry and have children—surely your wife has a right to know if her husband…'

'Isn't likely to live to see them grow up?' he slotted in without expression. 'There will be no wife and no children. The Carreras name will live on through Antonio and Katerina.'

'I thought you were many things, but a coward wasn't one of them,' she admitted.

Raul's taut profile clenched even tighter as he drew a

deep breath. 'I do not wish to discuss this with you, and you will not mention this to my mother.'

'What do you take me for?' she gasped.

'Also you will not encourage my mother to take you to Spain.'

Nell blinked. *'Me?'* She released an incredulous laugh.

Raul, who had pushed his fingers through his thick dark hair and risen to his feet in a fluid motion that made her indiscriminate stomach muscles quiver in appreciation, ignored her acid interjection totally.

'You can't go to Spain with my mother. You will not encourage her in this.' Having reached the far end of the room, he turned abruptly and pinned her with a penetrating stare. 'Is that understood?'

This arrogant pronouncement made Nell, who had been about to say they finally were in agreement over something, bite her tongue. 'This is probably just me...' she flashed him an apologetic smile of biblically insincere proportions '...but I was under the impression you'd brought me here for the express purpose of getting me to do just that. You really do take the cake; you set me up and then you throw a wobbler because things are going the way you planned. *You* planned,' she tacked on in a voice that trembled with anger.

'I am not throwing a "wobbler,"' he bit back. 'And I did not plan for you to go to Spain with my mother. I want you *here*.'

'What's the difference where I am, so long as I'm doing what you want?'

'I want you here,' he repeated with even more bullish emphasis. 'Where I can keep an eye on you.' *Where I can touch, smell and see you.*

Nell's eyes widened in disbelief—he really was incredible. 'In case I suddenly get the urge to make off with the family silver, you mean.'

'Do not be stupid.'

His dismissive contempt made Nell see red, or maybe, she mused vaguely, that was the headache that had been steadily getting worse all evening. She fixed her eyes on her trembling fingers twisted together on the table-top before getting to her feet. A throb of pain in her temple made Nell grimace and grab hold of the back of the chair to steady herself.

'What is wrong? Are you ill?'

Nell lifted a hand to shade her eyes from the glare of the light. 'I have a headache,' she admitted faintly.

'I have never seen anyone look like that with a headache,' Raul observed harshly after he examined the contours of her white face.

'It might be a migraine.'

'Might be or is?'

'Is,' she admitted.

He rolled his eyes. 'Why on earth didn't you say so sooner? I will call a doctor.'

'Please don't fuss. I don't need a doctor, just a dark quiet room and...' She released an anguished moan as an extra sharp stab of pain lanced through her skull. She felt so wretched she didn't protest as he scooped her up into his arms. She was vaguely conscious of him quietly issuing instructions in Spanish to someone as they went upstairs. She was grateful everyone was speaking quietly.

Her gratitude proved to be premature. 'What are you doing with her?' a voice that hurt Nell's throbbing head demanded shrilly.

'Lower your voice, Katerina.'

'Kate, I've got a migraine.' Nell tried to smile to reassure the girl. Opening her eyes hurt. 'Go back to bed.' She closed her eyes again, feeling too wretched to worry about whether she did.

'I can manage now, thank you,' she said as Raul deposited her on the bed.

He frowned doubtfully. 'Are you sure?'

'Definitely. I just need sleep. Please go away!' she begged.

She expected him to argue, mainly because that was what he did, so when she opened her eyes again a little while later and found herself alone she was surprised. Under the circumstances it was perverse to feel deserted.

Half an hour later Raul knocked on the door and when there was no reply he entered. The room was illuminated by a single soft lamp, and it was empty. The pyjamas he had asked the maid to bring were lying across the empty rumpled bed. There was a trail of garments leading to the bathroom door.

Cursing softly under his breath, he followed the trail. The door of the bathroom was ajar. Nell was sitting on the edge of the bath wearing nothing but a bra and pants. Her hands were in the washbasin; her fingertips trailed in the water gurgling from the open tap.

He dropped down on his knees beside her. 'Nell?'

Her heavy, dark-rimmed eyes opened; he was relieved when recognition supplanted the initial lack of acknowledgement in the shadowed depths.

'What are you doing?' she asked.

'Ringing an ambulance, I think.' He touched her arm; it felt like ice. Her skin had a marble-like pallor and perspiration stood out across her forehead and beaded her upper lip.

'Don't be such a drama queen. I look much worse than I feel. Actually feel much better now I've been sick.' At least he hadn't witnessed her throwing up. 'That's the way it works. I was just having a little rest here before I went back to bed.'

'How did you plan on getting there…on your hands and knees?' He picked up a face cloth and, after running it under the warm water, applied it to her face and neck.

'That's nice,' she admitted, leaning her head back against the support of the hand he had placed at the back of her neck. 'You shouldn't be doing this.'

'Why not?'

'Because…'

'I can see it kills you to admit it, but you need help.'

'Maybe that girl who brought me the night clothes could…'

'She's in bed. Everyone is in bed; you're stuck with me.'

Nell's train of thought was broken when he scooped her up into his arms. With a sigh she linked her arms about his neck, too tired to protest.

'Let's get you to your bed. Not quite the way I planned to,' he added to himself in a self-derisive undertone.

'You planned to get me in bed?'

'You weren't meant to hear that,' he replied, pulling the quilt up to her chin.

Nell sighed as the light was extinguished. Despite the silence she was gripped by the strong conviction she was not alone. 'Are you still there?'

'Yes,' came the reply from the darkness.

'You don't have to stay.'

'I know.' Raul arranged his tall frame into the chair beside the bed.

CHAPTER TEN

NELL sat up with a start. She looked around her opulent surroundings with a blank expression of confusion.

'Did I wake you?' a small voice asked.

The previous evening's events came zooming back, as did the headache, not in the same apocalyptic proportions of the previous night, but a steady, dull throb just behind her eyes. Nell lifted a hand to her temple, and smiled at the small figure sitting cross-legged on the bottom of her bed.

'No, you didn't wake me. How long have you been there?'

'Not long.'

Nell reached out and touched Antonio's bare toes. 'Long enough; you're freezing.' She turned back the quilt and patted the bed. 'Get in.'

A slow grin split the gravity of the little boy's face as he did as she suggested.

'Better?' she asked, tucking the quilt in around him.

He gave a nod and a little sigh of contentment. 'Uncle Raul said you were staying with us?' Nell was concerned by the anxiety she could see in the serious dark eyes that scanned her face.

Uncle Raul playing his trump card or Uncle Raul comforting a needy child? In the end Raul's machinations were irrelevant; the only thing that actually mattered was that Antonio needed her. 'Then if Uncle Raul says so, I guess I am.'

She felt some of the tension ease out of his skinny body as he curled up contentedly against her. 'I like Uncle Raul.'

'That's good.'

'He does cool things with me, and he listens when I say stuff, which most people don't because I'm a kid. I don't mean you, Nell.' A note of anxiety crept into his voice as he continued. 'Don't tell Kate I said I like him, will you? Promise,' he added fiercely.

'Not if you don't want me to, but why can't I tell Kate?' Nell asked gently.

'Kate doesn't like him. They fight. I hate it when people fight.' He sighed.

Nell felt herself fill with emotion. Poor, quiet, undemanding Antonio stuck in the middle. As he was not considered a problem his needs were in danger of being overlooked. She gave the little boy a hug. 'Oh, Antonio,' she sighed, kissing the top of his glossy head as she released him. 'You mustn't feel guilty for liking your uncle.'

'Do you like him?'

'He's not my uncle.'

'But do you *like* him? Kate said you didn't.'

She closed her eyes; it had to be genetic. She should have known better—Antonio might be a young boy, but he was still a Carreras male and as such not easily fobbed off.

Elbow wedged against the pillow, she propped her chin in her hand. 'I think your uncle loves you very much, Antonio, and I know he will keep you safe. How could I *not* like someone who will do that for my best boy?'

She was relieved to see that her response had satisfied Antonio, who looked happy.

'I seem to remember saying not to wake up Miss Rose.'

Nell's chin slipped inelegantly out of her cupped hand. She heard Antonio laugh as she tumbled face first into the pillow. With her head buried in percale-covered duck down she felt extremely reluctant to move. Moving would involve facing Raul and trying to behave like a moderately rational human being; not something, she knew from bitter experience, that was easy to do and on those previous occasions she hadn't been wearing just a bra and pants.

Oh, well, a bit late to be modest, she thought as an image of herself curled up in his arms popped into her head. Taking the quilt with her, she sat up, brushing her hair back from her face with her forearm.

Raul's eyes followed the progress of the burnished mass as her hair settled against her shoulders, his expression enigmatic. 'Sorry if I startled you. When Antonio goes missing he has a habit of turning up where he shouldn't be.' Beside her, Antonio squirmed. 'I didn't like to knock, I thought you might be sleeping, but...'

Nell listened politely even though the only question that she really wanted to hear an answer to was, *How long had he been standing there?*

'I didn't wake her, Uncle Raul. I was waiting for her to wake up, and she did.'

'So I see,' Raul observed drily. His attention turned to Nell. 'Are you feeling any better this morning?'

'Heaps,' she promised gruffly.

Her tension cranked up several notches as he came to stand within a foot of the bed. Her fingers plucked nervously at the sheet as she endured a clinical inspection of her upturned features.

'I always look this bad in the morning.'

'You look...' he paused, presumably moderating his language in front of the child before completing colourlessly '...tired.' His brow pleated. 'Do you get migraines often?'

To Nell he sounded disapproving of this weakness. 'Occasionally.'

'Have you sought medical advice?'

'That's not necessary. I don't get them that often and I normally carry medication for when it does happen. I'm really sorry if I caused you any inconvenience.'

'Are you a morning person, Uncle Raul?'

'A morning person?'

'Dad said that Nell is a morning person. He wasn't,' he added matter-of-factly. 'He was cranky in the morning. Wasn't he, Nell?'

'Unapproachable before his second cup of coffee,' she confirmed. Still smiling slightly, she switched her attention back to Raul and was confused to see anger smouldering in his eyes in the moment before the screen of his dark lashes came down.

'Come, Antonio, your breakfast is ready.'

'But I want—'

'Now, Antonio. Let Miss Rose rest.'

His expression was hidden from her but there was nothing in his voice or manner that suggested he was angry. He didn't raise his voice; he didn't need to. Antonio responded with only a token grumble to the command. Maybe she had been mistaken about what she had seen?

Nell's attention was drawn to his fingers tapping against the quilt. His hand looked very dark against the pale bed linen and watching his long fingers stroke the fabric made her stomach muscles clutch. The action was mundane, but somehow the sensuality that was very much an integral part of him was reflected in the simple action.

Raul watched as the child twined his stick-like arms around Nell's neck and pressed a resounding kiss to her lips.

Antonio's enthusiasm sent the quilt slithering to the floor as he leapt out of bed. It was pretty irrational feeling exposed when the only person who might be looking at her had seen her that way the night before, but Nell lifted her knees to her chin, hugging her legs to her body.

At the door the boy stopped and turned back.

'You will be here when I get home from school?'

'Absolutely,' Nell promised. Her smile faded and she sighed as the door closed behind him. She rested her chin on her knees and wrapped her arms tighter around her legs.

'Are you really feeling better?' asked Raul.

Nell turned her face to one side to look at him. 'A bit sore, but otherwise back to normal. You…you were kind last night.'

'Mother will be pleased you are well—she was concerned. She is sure it is my fault for arguing with you.'

'It's more a multi-factor thing, and stress is one of those factors, but don't get the hair shirt out just yet—you are only one stress-inducing factor in my life.'

He didn't reply; he just continued to look at her with a driven intensity that was deeply unnerving. 'Antonio is very like his father, do you not think?'

Nell nodded. 'Yes, he is.'

'You miss Javier?'

'Of course,' she replied, her thoughts still very much with his son. 'As you must,' she added.

Raul, his strong jaw clenched tight, surveyed her delicate, pensive profile. 'What a women feels for a man is hardly the same as a man feels for his brother,' he commented harshly.

'I suppose not,' she conceded.

'You have decided to stay?'

'Do I have much choice?' she asked him drily.

One dark brow elevated as his eyes swept over her face. 'There is always a choice.' His eyes narrowed shrewdly on her frowning face. 'You don't think this is going to work, do you?'

'Do you? I mean, with the way you feel about me, how can it? I mean, you obviously can't stand being in the same room as me.'

He made no attempt to deny her husky assessment. 'This house has a lot of rooms. I think we might manage not to share one too often. Now, if you'll excuse me...'

His suggestion was practical; it ought to have made her feel a lot happier. So why was she left feeling vaguely disgruntled as she watched him disappear through the door without another word?

CHAPTER ELEVEN

THOUGH Nell had broached the subject on several occa
sions, nobody had spelt out what was expected of her. The
only advice she received was to relax and enjoy herself
Nell knew that Aria meant it kindly, but she seriousl
doubted if Raul would be pleased if she swanned around
as if she were on holiday, though in actual fact the
Carrerases' London home was a lot more luxurious than
any holiday resort she had ever stayed at.

Nell was determined not to give him any opportunity to
complain she was acting like a sponger. She might not be
employed in any official capacity, but she resolved to make
herself useful. In this resolve she was rather more success
ful than she had bargained for.

Obviously she was available for the children wheneve
they might need her, but when the staff, reluctant to bothe
Aria while her health was not good, approached an embar
rassed Nell she explained she didn't have that sort of role
in the house. It was only after Aria said she would be
happy, in fact grateful, if Nell acted on her behalf when
small matters that required a decision arose, that Nell be
came involved.

'It wouldn't be often,' the older woman reassured her
'The housekeeper is extremely capable and the butler, as
I'm sure you've already seen, a model of efficiency, but
very occasionally conflicts arise and someone is needed to
pour oil on troubled waters.'

So if Nell had imagined she would have a lot of time on
her hands now that the centre had been closed, she was

rapidly disabused of this notion. Her days had never been busier.

Katerina and Antonio quickly became involved in a bewildering variety of after-school activities and classes. Getting anywhere meant driving around the traffic-locked city, a time-consuming and frequently frustrating task.

When Antonio's new school, keen to involve parents in school activities, approached the children's grandmother to ask did she have any special skills she might like to contribute to school life, it was Nell who found herself volunteering to help out in the art department.

Over the weeks she took on any number of other tasks, including painting scenery for the end-of-term concert at Katerina's school. Helping with homework—anything except maths!—was par for the course, but occasionally something more demanding cropped up, like bundling Katerina to the hairdresser's when a home-colouring experiment went disastrously wrong before her uncle could see his niece's green hair.

Although at times she felt restless—peculiarly these bouts often followed the odd occasions when she had contact with Raul—Nell was actually happy with what she was doing, and thought everyone else was too until she found Raul waiting for her one morning after she had completed the school run.

Normally he was out of the house at half-past seven and rarely returned before seven in the evening. By that time Nell had already eaten dinner with Katerina and Antonio. The weekends he kept free for the children and, though she had been invited to join in at first on their excursions, she had known Raul expected her to refuse—not that he showed any signs of appreciation when she followed his guidelines to the letter and came up with some excuse.

When she recognised the unmistakable silhouette of his

tall, broad-shouldered figure through the glass panel that separated the porch from the elegant entrance hall tension slid through her. She checked out her reflection in the glass only to almost immediately ask herself, *What's the point?* To Raul she was part of the furniture, only warranting attention when she didn't function efficiently—like a broken table.

Seeing herself as the human equivalent of a wonky chair was not an ego-enhancing exercise. It took Nell several moments of fierce concentration before she could compose herself enough to enter.

Disguising the effect he had on her was becoming increasingly difficult, and although she did her best to avoid being in the same room as him unfortunately sometimes it was impossible—as now.

Shoulders back, head at a jaunty angle, she walked into the hall; the cheery whistle she suspected was probably a bit of overkill, but in for a penny…? She took several steps, then pretended to see him for the first time.

Her smile might have lacked conviction but his was non-existent. It was then she noticed he was still wearing his black dinner jacket and bow-tie, though this was unfastened, as was his top button, revealing a tiny rectangular portion of brown skin. Her fixed smile guttered.

She assumed he was still seeing the lovely Roxie; the longevity of the attachment had caused excitement in the press. However, this inescapable evidence that he had not come home last night, that he had spent the night with her, brought the reality crashing home.

Some hitherto masochistic streak in her nature made her visualise him coming here straight from his lover's bed…with the scent of her still on his body. A violent shudder of revulsion passed through her body as her face paled.

'Where have you been?' he demanded roughly.

His accusatory tone made her blink. 'I dropped the children off at school.' Why was she jealous? It wasn't as if she wanted to be where the actress was… *Not much!*

With a frown he consulted his watch. 'Until this time?'

'The traffic was heavy.' Actually it had been lighter than usual that morning.

'Why are you taking the children to school? I employ a chauffeur. My mother would hardly require the car at this time of the morning, so don't try and tell me George was not available.'

George was always available. It seemed the height of extravagance to Nell to keep a full-time chauffeur when the only thing he did was take Aria to the odd lunch date or occasionally the shops. Raul himself, she knew, preferred to drive himself in one of the high-powered sleek cars he kept in the underground garage.

'I wasn't going to.'

Her politeness seemed to increase his displeasure. 'I will have a word with George,' he announced with his usual decisive air. Did he ever suffer from the doubts that plagued normal folk? she wondered enviously. 'To drive around the city during the rush hour requires skill and patience.'

'I'm a very good driver!' Nell protested, indignant at this slight on her driving skills.

He seemed to be going out of his way to be unpleasant. In fact, she mused, noticing for the first time tell-tale signs of strain evident in his lean, patrician face, he seemed really uptight. Had he and Roxie had a lovers' tiff?

Nothing too minor, she secretly hoped.

'That is not the point…' Obviously about to tell her what the point was, he stopped scanning her face with a brooding scowl. 'What is wrong?'

She pulled off the woollen cloche she had crammed on

over her recalcitrant curls and shoved it in the pocket of her jacket. She saw Raul's eyes move to her bright head, noticing no doubt that she was having a bad-hair day. Did someone as physically perfect as him, the sort of person who was incapable of performing a graceless action, understand about such things? she wondered.

'It's just cold outside,' she said, wrapping her arms tightly around herself and giving a convincing shiver. 'It really wouldn't be a good idea to ask George to drive the children,' she added, belatedly recalling his intention.

'And is there a reason why it wouldn't be a good idea? Beyond the fact you seem unable to sit still for more than ten seconds at a time.'

She let this accusation of hyperactivity, coming ironically from someone who was a world-class workaholic, pass.

'Kate doesn't want to be dropped off at school by a chauffeur-driven Rolls.' Raul looked at her blankly and Nell gave an exasperated sigh. 'You can be *so* dense sometimes.' She was immediately aware that her candour was not appreciated.

'Then, taking into account my lack of understanding,' Raul suggested with biting satire, 'perhaps you should spell out just what the hell you're talking about.'

'She's embarrassed.'

Raul shook his dark head. *'Embarrassed?'*

'Do you remember *anything* about being a teenager? Don't you recall the need to be accepted…be the same as everyone else?' She met his uncomprehending and impatient eyes. A dry laugh was drawn from her. 'No, of course you don't.' Why would he? Raul Carreras was not a pack animal, he was not part of the herd, he was the leader, a loner, aloof and supremely indifferent to the opinion of others.

'I thought teenagers wanted to express their own individuality…?'

'Teenagers want to be accepted by a group,' Nell contradicted confidently. 'The one thing above all others that your average teenager cannot bear,' she explained, 'is being different. The other girls don't get dropped off in a Rolls-Royce. A four-wheel drive, maybe,' she conceded, thinking of all the mums who amazingly seemed to consider a massive four-wheel drive off-roader essential for negotiating Kensington! 'And even if they did, unlike you, Kate wasn't brought up with the "if you've got it flaunt it" mentality.'

There was a long silence while Raul stared at her. 'And you think I…*flaunt* it?'

Though his tone was flat, remarkable for a lack of emotion rather than an excess, there was something there that made Nell suspect she had offended him. *Yet again!*

'Well, I *did*,' Nell admitted frankly. 'But you're not flash.' No, Raul was quite simply class.

'Thank you.' Though his manner was grave, there was a faint quiver in his deep voice.

'I realise now that you don't even think about appearances. Your motivation for driving expensive cars and nice clothes isn't to have people look at you. You don't actually care what other people think about you.'

He didn't deny this mildly wistful observation. 'But Katerina does?'

'That hardly makes her unique.'

'And you would have me believe that having money makes Katerina feel uncomfortable…?'

Nell could understand his scepticism; it must be hard for someone brought up with the proverbial silver spoon in his mouth to appreciate how people not used to that lifestyle might find it hard to adjust to.

She nodded. 'And a bit guilty.'

'Guilty?' he ejaculated. His dark gaze swept over her heart-shaped face. He thrust his hands into his pockets as the impulse to take that face between his hands became all-consuming. 'Are you sure you are not just endowing her with your own overdeveloped social conscience?'

'I don't have an overdeveloped social conscience.'

'No...?' One dark brow rose. 'You are the biggest sucker for a hard-luck story I've ever seen,' he condemned.

'I'm not!'

'What about the homeless guy you gave money to who turned around and stole your wallet and phone, then for good measure knocked you down...?' The story casually related by his nephew had made Raul's blood boil, and he hadn't even been able to relieve his feelings by laying violent hands on the vermin who had performed the cowardly deed.

Nell's eyes went wide with astonishment. The incident he described had happened a couple of years earlier. 'How on earth...? And he didn't knock me down, he gave a little push and I fell over.'

Raul gave a groan and pushed his fingers into his dark hair before ripping the unfastened tie from his neck and throwing it onto the desk. Muttering under his breath in Spanish, he stalked over to the window.

Nell watched his progress covertly from under the sweep of her lashes. The way he moved brought a sleek jungle cat to mind...an *angry* sleek jungle cat, she mentally amended as he spun around and pinned her with blazing and furious black eyes.

'That's *exactly* what I mean. You are a soft touch, no— you are a soft touch with very little judgement. In fact you are not fit to be let out without a minder!' he contended grimly.

His unwarranted and rancorous attack made her blanch.

She knew he didn't like her, that she irritated him, but it seemed he actually hated her, she thought miserably. She had started thinking lately that anything from him would be better than the polite indifference she had been receiving. She was wrong.

This cleared up the mystery of why he had been avoiding her—he obviously couldn't stand the sight of her. *Well, bang goes the theory that he is actually struggling to hide a growing attraction.* There was wishful thinking and then again there was gross stupidity.

'Aren't you losing track here? We were talking about Kate.'

Raul looked at her blankly. *'What?'*

Her brows lifted. 'Your niece.'

Twin dark bands of colour appeared along the slant of his sculpted cheekbones.

'Don't worry, I'm sure she'll get used to being part of a wealthy dynasty. Actually,' Nell added, thinking wryly of how easy she had found it to take very much for granted the touches of luxury that had seemed like the height of decadence when she had moved in, 'she'll get to like it.'

'So I should not offer to drive them to school myself?'

'That would be different. You're...'

One dark brow rose quizzically. 'I am...?'

Nell blushed. 'Well, let's just say it would do no teenage girl's reputation any harm to be seen getting out of a car driven by you.'

'Is that a compliment?'

Nell dragged her thoughts away from the devastating charm of his smile. 'Just a comment on the shallowness of your average teenage girl. Now, did you want me for anything else?' she asked with a hunted look at the elegantly curving stairs.

Raul's eyes saw the direction of her gaze and correctly

interpreted her desire to escape. His lips twisted into a self-derisive smile. 'I want you…'

Nell's tummy flipped. Heart hammering, breath trapped in her tight chest, she slowly turned her head. The muscles along Raul's jaw tightened as he returned her stare.

'In the library.'

Chastising herself for letting her imagination run away with her, and feeling uncomfortably like a pupil summoned to the headmaster's office, Nell followed him. Raul, courteous but cold, stood to one side to allow a maid carrying a great pile of glossy magazines and the latest financial periodicals to enter ahead of them.

Nell could see that the boss's presence was making the poor girl, who she knew had only been working here for a few weeks, nervous. Small wonder she was, Nell thought, angling a meaningful frown towards Raul, who stood there, impatience radiating from every elegant line of his imposing figure. Couldn't he see she was scared stiff of him? Well, if he did he was making no attempt to put her at her ease.

It didn't seem to register with Raul when the girl knocked a fragile—probably priceless—figurine off the bureau with her elbow. She looked as though she was going to burst into tears. Nell took pity on her.

'Gloria, give those to me,' she demanded, hefting the girl's burden into her own arms. 'And don't worry, I'll get rid of the old ones for you. How did the party go? Did John turn up?'

Gloria gave a conspiratorial grin. 'Yes, and *she* was livid because he didn't even look at her…'

Her employer clearing his throat noisily prevented Nell hearing the rest of this girlish confidence. The girl shot an apologetic look in Raul's direction. Her smile for Nell held sympathy as she ducked out of the room.

'What do you think you're doing?' Raul demanded icily as Nell began to arrange the magazines on the table in neat piles.

'What does it look like?' She didn't glance in his direction, but as she continued to fuss she could feel the invisible rays of his disapproval and impatience boring into her back.

'Will you stop that, woman?'

Nell had finished, but his terse tone perversely made her rearrange things once more, slowly and precisely.

'Did you hear what I said?'

'Yes.'

She heard the harsh sound of his angry inhalation, but did not regret her provocative behaviour. Life was bad enough as it was, but if he got the idea that all he had to do was click his fingers and she would jump life really would be unbearable. She had so little control of other aspects of her life, namely being so forcefully attracted to a man who regarded her as an irritant, that it felt important to show she did have a choice about other things.

Nell let out a startled cry of protest when, without warning, Raul stepped forward and bodily lifted her away as if she weighed nothing. Having casually planted her several feet away, he positioned himself directly in front of her. Then without breaking eye contact he lifted his arm and knocked the magazines she had taken so much care with flying across the room.

She looked at the mess on the floor and gave a derisive little sniff. 'Do you feel better now?'

The words snagged in her throat as she looked up at him. He really was stunning, she reflected with an inward sigh as she drank in the details: golden skin drawn taut over slashing cheekbones, that wide, sensual mouth and his incredible extravagantly dark eyes that were shimmering with anger.

With an effort she focused her thoughts. 'If you've had a rough night, don't take it out on me. I have to tell you a grown man having a full-blown temper tantrum is not a pretty sight.'

She stooped down to pick up a magazine that had landed at her feet.

'It is not your job to pick things up,' he growled. 'I employ people to do that.'

Nell rose gracefully to her feet. 'I have hands.' She held them out palm up to demonstrate the fact. 'I am not incapable,' she told him scornfully. 'When I drop things I pick them up myself. I don't ring for someone else to do it for me.'

'That is not what I meant.'

'Then what did you mean?'

He glowered at her with every appearance of intense dislike. 'Must you gossip with the servants? It is not appropriate,' he told her severely. 'You make them uncomfortable.'

'I wasn't gossiping, I was talking, trying to put the poor girl at her ease. You were the one terrifying her.'

'I do not scare people,' he said through gritted teeth, looking as though he would dearly like to throttle her.

'What about poor Gloria? She was shaking, poor girl.'

'Who is Gloria?'

'You are terrible.'

After a few moments of mutual glaring Nell sighed; honesty made her unable to ignore the facts. It was impossible for her to live in the house for as long as she had without recognising that he was a good and reasonable employer who was always meticulously polite to his staff and treated them with a respect that was returned.

'I know you don't do it deliberately,' she admitted. 'It's just your manner. It can be a little bit daunting.'

His narrowed eyes swept her face with an expression of frustration. 'Pity it doesn't work on you,' he retorted testily.

This uncharacteristically childish retort made her stare. She watched as he took a deep breath and smoothed back the rumpled hair from his brow. The details of something as simple as the shape of his hands and the fine, tapering length of his long, sensitive fingers were endlessly fascinating to her.

'However, that is not why I wish to speak to you.'

Nell dragged her attention back to his face. He just stared at her; there was a dangerous, explosive quality to his dark, brooding regard.

She was relieved when he broke the nerve-shredding silence.

'I did not realise, until my mother told me, how much you have taken on.'

'*Taken on?*' she echoed with a puzzled frown.

'You are not expected to spend your entire day running around after Antonio and Katerina, and there is no need for you to sit and read aloud to my mother for hours or sort out domestic crises.'

'I *enjoy* reading aloud to your mother,' Nell protested.

He dismissed her protest with a movement of his hand. 'That is not what I intended when I asked you to move in.'

'What, me enjoy myself?'

He slid her a look that made her flush.

'It is not appropriate that you are on call around the clock.'

'Hardly that! I've loads of time to myself. Antonio and Kate are at school most of the time.'

'You take them there and pick them up, and in between are being used as an unpaid helper at school,' he declared disapprovingly.

'It's a good idea for parents to be involved,' she protested.

'You are not a parent.'

Nell flinched. 'Oh, I see.'

She did, and she was totally mortified that it had taken her this long to catch on. Raul had been trying to tell her that she was overstepping the mark, that she had been encroaching in areas where she was not wanted. She wasn't the children's mother; she wasn't even paid help!

He was right, of course; it was wrong of her to allow the children to become reliant on her. She wasn't going to be here for ever.

A flicker of concern entered Raul's eyes as he studied her face. 'You understand what I am saying?'

Nell swallowed and lifted her chin. 'Absolutely,' she replied with a resolute little smile.

'You need some leisure time.'

CHAPTER TWELVE

WHICH sounded very generous, but as far as Nell was concerned was nothing but a polite way of saying, Remember your place and keep your distance—which was why at that moment Nell was swimming laps in the private indoor pool.

The next time Raul asked her she would be able to supply evidence that she had been following his instructions.

Nell had just about finished doing her laps when she became aware that she was not alone. She swam to the side of the pool and, hands braced on the tiled pool-edge, levered herself out—or at least tried to. Her arms felt weak after the unaccustomed exertion and it took her two attempts to heave herself out of the water.

'Hi there.'

Nell, lying face down in an ungainly heap, feeling very like the human version of a beached whale on the tiled surface, stared at the long, slim legs of the woman standing beside her.

'Miss…' Nell scrambled into an upright position, taking the towel the blonde handed her with a small smile of thanks.

The actress didn't comment on the greeting; obviously her fame was such she took such recognition very much for granted.

'You must be the nanny.' Her curiosity as she examined the younger woman's face and figure was quite unself-conscious.

Nell, who never had quite defined what her role in the Carreras household was, didn't correct her.

'So using the pool is a perk of the job.'

Nell, who would have been quick to pick up such things, could not detect any condescension in her friendly manner.

'This is quite a set-up, isn't it?' Roxie continued, gazing around the lavish pool area, which came complete with columns, waterfall and spa pool. Her Grecian-inspired gown, one-shouldered and virtually backless, was rather appropriate for the décor. 'And you swim really well,' she added generously.

'Thank you.' Not only stunningly beautiful, nice too—a real sickener.

'It made me tired just watching you.'

'I like the water.' And swimming yourself into exhaustion made it easier to sleep. At least in theory.

So this was the sort of woman Raul found attractive. The actress was actually much more attractive in the flesh than on the screen. She was also much thinner and had the longest legs that Nell had ever seen, made even longer by the incredibly high heels she was wearing at the moment. Barely topping five two in her bare feet, dripping wet and wearing a black swimming costume that was utilitarian rather than fashionable, Nell felt at a distinct disadvantage.

Nell usually found exercise left her feeling pretty upbeat but on this occasion there was no post-work-out high, just an oppressive cloud of gloom over her head.

'I love swimming too; it's great for your boobs,' Roxie explained, making a breast-stroke motion in the air.

It didn't seem to Nell as her eyes automatically slid over the perky contours of the actress's generous breasts that she needed any help in that area. Hers, on the other hand, she thought, glancing miserably at her own moderate-sized breasts flattened by the Lycra of her swimsuit, could do with a bit of help.

'The problem with swimming is the chemicals in the water,' the actress continued earnestly.

Nell tried to look interested as Roxie went on to explain in an authoritative manner about the additives that were put in pool water; she included a good deal of technical information about PH factors.

'I didn't know that,' Nell admitted. Beautiful and not dumb...though maybe slightly boring? She immediately felt mean for the catty thought.

'It plays havoc with coloured hair, don't you find?' Roxie asked, her eyes fixed on the wet-darkened red strands that Nell was towelling dry. 'I love that shade you have, by the way.'

'It's actually red when it's dry,' Nell admitted.

'I know. I saw you the other day taking the kids out. We waved, but you didn't see us.'

'Oh, really.' Actually there had been no 'we'. Raul hadn't waved, just his blonde companion, and Nell had studiously pretended not to see them. She felt as if her guilt was written all over her face.

'You know, you shouldn't wear baggy sweaters with a waist like that.' Pale blue eyes focused on Nell's narrow waist and flat, trim tummy.

'I'll try and remember.'

'And use a protective serum on your hair. I had an awful experience when I went swimming at Cannes. My hair went orange...honestly, totally orange!' She shuddered at the memory. 'Leo flew straight out, of course, and he was livid with me.'

'Mine's natural,' Nell cut in apologetically.

The other girl's eyes widened. 'You're kidding!' she exclaimed. 'No highlights?' Nell shook her head. 'Low lights?' Roxie shook her head in amazement. 'Incredible! If you ever do fancy having a change...' Head on one side, she weighed up an increasingly uncomfortable Nell with a expert eye. 'You'd really look good blonde, you know.'

'I don't think—' Nell began.

'No, trust me on this, you'd look great, and if you men tion my name to Leo—he's my colourist and the only on I'd let touch mine—' she lifted a complacent hand to h honey-blonde head '—he'd fit you in as a favour to me She stopped, a slow smile spreading over her breathtaking lovely features as her gaze drifted to a point somewhe over Nell's shoulder.

'Raul, darling,' the actress cried as she ran towards th approaching figure.

Nell, who had no desire whatever to witness the deligh she'd seen on the other woman's face expressed in a mo physical form, kept her back turned to them and hasti pulled her towel protectively around herself.

'I interrupted her swim,' she heard Roxie say as the reached the spot where she was standing, every muscle her body poised for flight.

'I didn't know you were swimming.'

Being directly addressed meant she could no long avoid looking at him. Her breath caught in her throat. Ra might have more confidence than she considered acceptab in a man, but she had to admit he did have some justi cation! He looked totally sensational! Elegant to his fi gertips in a way that didn't detract one jot from his ra masculinity, dressed in an immaculately tailored suit, Ra presented a picture guaranteed to instantly arouse lust the female breast.

Well, hers at least.

Roxie was his male equivalent. Him dark, and her d vinely fair. A combination of their genes would make i credibly beautiful children. Was it something they'd di cussed?

Why do this to yourself, Nell?

Chin up, she took a deep breath and angrily drew a veil cross this line of speculation.

'I did ask your mother whether it was all right,' Nell esponded defensively, aware in the periphery of her vision f Roxie laying her head against Raul's shoulder.

A spasm of annoyance twisted Raul's mouth. 'There is o need for you to *ask* anyone. Have I not made myself lear on that score?' he demanded. 'Is something wrong ith the air-conditioning in here?' he added abruptly.

'Not that I know,' Nell replied with a sneaking suspicion f where he was heading.

'It feels pretty warm to me, darling,' Roxie added.

'That's because it is meant to be kept at a constant hu- idified eighty-four,' he added, his significant stare coming o rest on Nell, who was cocooned from head to toe in owelling. 'I take it there is some reason for this display of nodesty?'

Roxie's splutter of laughter drew Raul's attention from hot-cheeked Nell. 'Sorry, darling, but if you'd seen her wim suit...' She shot Nell an apologetic glance. 'I've valked through town showing more than she is.'

The lines around Raul's eyes deepened with affectionate varmth as he looked down at the woman beside him. 'But hen it's not what you wear, but how you wear it.'

Nell's response was pretty much what any female's vould be if someone implied she didn't have class or style. Ie hadn't come right out and said it, of course, but the mplication was obvious. *Well, I might be able to wear lothes if I had a personal stylist and designers just begging ne to wear their latest creations!*

'It's very bad to let your muscles get cold after exercise,' Iell explained coldly.

'Well, you look much more likely to succumb to hea
stroke,' Raul observed sardonically.

Roxie, with an exasperated cry, curled her fingers aroun
Raul's strong, masculine jaw and turned his head firml
back towards her. With her free hand she stroked his sleev
'Will you stop teasing the poor girl, Raul?' There was
sexy huskiness that hadn't been in her voice when she'
spoken to Nell. '*I'm* the one you've kept hanging aroun
half the evening waiting for you,' she reminded him.

'Tell me why I'm going to this party again?'

'No more calls?'

'Not at the moment.' Raul put a hand on the smaller on
that was stroking his arm and brought it deliberately to hi
lips. As his head lifted he looked directly at Nell. The taun
ing smile almost instantly left his lips and concern fille
his eyes.

Her deathly pallor extended even to her lips; the intens
blue of her wide-spaced eyes supplied the only scrap c
colour that was in her face. It seemed to him that she wa
on the verge of passing out. He tensed, fully expecting *
be required to catch her when she fell.

Nell deliberately let her towel drop to the floor. Bendin
forward to pick it up sent the blood rushing back to he
oxygen-starved brain. The action had been instinctive. *
dormant protective instinct awakening in a moment of ex
treme need. She had been totally unprepared for the vic
lence of the revulsion she had felt when Raul had touche
the other woman.

Though outwardly composed as she straightened up, in
side she felt the knife-thrust of jealousy cutting into vita
areas of her anatomy. She had not known that such ex
tremes of emotion existed, let alone suspected that she wa
capable of experiencing them. Like the final piece in a jig
saw, everything slotted into place—you could only keep u

the pretence that something wasn't happening for just so long. She had fallen for him. She had fallen for Raul Carreras!

'I got bored waiting for you so I thought I'd explore,' Roxie was explaining to Raul.

'So I see.'

Raul did not seem to be an overly demonstrative lover, which, considering she'd almost passed out when he had touched the other woman's hand, was possibly a blessing! Perhaps, she mused, he kept his demonstrations for the privacy of the bedroom? Nell closed her eyes willing the erotic images of intimately entwined sweat-drenched bodies to go away.

'Actually I was just saying to…? Sorry, I don't know your name.'

When Nell didn't respond it was Raul who supplied the information.

'Nell.'

Nell jolted free of the imagined scene of seduction that was playing in her head, opened her eyes and collided with Raul's implacable stare. Suddenly, totally convinced that her hopeless longing was written as clear as neon on her face—what other reason could there be for the inexplicable strain stamped on his own dark features?—she was gripped by a frantic desire to escape.

'Have a nice evening,' she muttered indistinctly. Her rigid facial muscles ached with the effort of smiling.

'You don't need to go on our account. We're on our way to a party, and I make it a point to be late. Though not,' Roxie added, tapping Raul playfully on the arm, 'as late as this, usually.'

Despite this pointed reminder Raul did not respond. His eyes continued to follow Nell's movements.

'No, I'm all swum out,' Nell promised hoarsely.

'Raul, I was just telling…Nell—' she gifted Nell one of her truly dazzling smiles '—to go see my colourist. With her colouring she'd just look incredible blonde.' She smiled at the younger girl warmly. 'Blondes have the most fun, I promise you.' She cast Raul a sultry look from under her long, curling lashes. 'Come on, honey, back me up here.'

Raul was looking at Nell. 'No!' he said flatly.

The word stopped Nell in her tracks. She stood there poised for flight like a rabbit caught in the headlights.

The actress frowned at Raul. 'Why shouldn't she go blonde if she wants?'

'I don't want…' Nell began, longing to be anywhere but here. The air-conditioning couldn't regulate the atmosphere of growing tension in the room.

'She is not going blonde.'

'Not platinum or anything, much more subtle a—'

'She is *not* touching her hair.'

This autocratic decree made the actress look indignant on Nell's behalf. 'Just because the girl works for you…'

'She doesn't,' Raul slotted in without taking his eyes off Nell's face.

The actress looked from one to the other with a thoughtful expression. 'Then what does she do?' She gave a slightly puzzled smile. 'Other than swim.'

Nell's body sagged as Raul's eyes finally left her face. His devouring gaze had left her weak as a kitten.

'She is a guest here.'

The actress's skilfully enhanced pale eyes widened. 'Oh, I *see*.' There was a wealth of understanding in the sentence.

A wave of scalding heat passed over Nell's skin. It was obvious to see what the older woman was thinking. Even worse was her apparent casual acceptance of the situation. Nell couldn't imagine herself having the sort of relationship where the strongest emotion you experienced on learning of your lover's infidelities was curiosity!

If it had happened to me? A grim expression settled on her soft features as she contemplated her response to such a betrayal. Then, belatedly conscious that her prolonged silence might be interpreted as an admission, she summoned an amused smile.

'No, it's not like that at all!'

She turned her attention to Raul, her expression inviting him to intercede and explain the circumstances that had brought her here. He just stood there, looking if anything faintly bored.

'I lived with Raul's brother.' The reminder made Raul frown darkly. 'I'm here to help the children settle in.'

Why is it the truth often sounds less plausible than a lie? Maybe because it was only part of the truth; deep down could she honestly say that her motives in moving in had been so entirely altruistic? Hadn't the fact that she would see Raul affected her decision?

'So you two aren't…?' Roxie looked from Nell to Raul and back again. She laughed. 'Oh, don't look so horrified, darling,' she told Nell. 'You're not at all his type. I could see that straight off,' she confided, apparently oblivious to the antagonistic glitter that had entered Nell's blue eyes.

'And he's not mine!' Nell said, gritting her teeth. *Except when he's nothing better to do than give me a glimpse of what I'm missing.*

'Well, honey, that makes you kind of unique,' the other woman purred, looking entertained by the younger girl's spitting declaration. 'But be careful. That's the sort of challenge some men can't resist,' she warned playfully. She tilted her head up to Raul. 'What do you say, darling?'

'I say it might be a good idea if you answer that phone,

Roxie.' Raul, his face set like stone, did not respond to his companion's raillery.

The blonde, not even slightly put out by his impatient attitude, pouted prettily and obligingly pulled out a slim phone, which had been ringing intermittently for the last five minutes from her tiny, beaded evening purse.

Nell, her face still burning with mortification at being the source of their amusement, gathered up her damp towel and the paperback she had planned to read. Without even looking at Raul she prepared to take her leave. A hand on her shoulder spun her back.

She shrank away from his touch and with a dark scowl Raul dropped his hand. 'What is wrong?' he demanded, his dark eyes raking her face.

He had not made any attempt to lower his voice and Nell, worried that he might say something that would embarrass her further in front of the other woman, glanced towards the far end of the pool where the actress had retreated to take her call. Not, if the volume of her voice was anything to go by, for privacy. Though listening in on a conversation that seemed to consist for the most part of a series of 'darling's in varying tones did not provide excitement for even the most dedicated eavesdropper.

'Nothing's wrong,' she hissed, clutching her belongings to her chest.

'Then why are you running away?' he drawled. 'And why did you almost pass out back there? Have you got a migraine?'

'I have not got a migraine. I never pass out and I'm not running away; I'm simply going back to my room.' She took a deep breath, no longer able to contain her anger. 'So if you want a floor show I suggest you go to a club,' she suggested, blinking away the tears that threatened to spill from her huge, accusing eyes. 'Call me peculiar, but I happen not to like being the butt of the joke for you and your friends,' she informed him coldly.

'I am not laughing at you.'

He wasn't.

It might have been easier to bear if he were. The intensity of his regard was far harder to bear than laughter. His hooded gaze slid hungrily down the length of her body. The contraction of the muscles in his brown throat as he swallowed was visible.

She was always painfully conscious in his presence of her body and her femininity in a way that made her feel awkward and excited simultaneously. Seeing him at any time made her body react; the casual brush of his eyes as they passed could make her nipples harden with longing. But this was no casual brush of his eyes; the challenge gleaming in his eyes was overtly sexual. The look said, *I want you.*

Heat flooded through her; she couldn't breathe. Literally weak with lust and longing, her knees shook. His dark face swam as her vision blurred.

If you pretended something wasn't happening, did it go away?

'I suppose you think I'm being oversensitive?' Her voice sounded strange, as though it were coming from a long way away.

'You are sensitive to my touch,' he rasped. 'You tremble when I touch you.'

'The same happens when I touch a live electric wire…at least it would do if I did, which I don't,' she added, some sense of her desperation seeping into her voice.

Raul moved his head in acknowledgement of her words. 'Electricity would describe it, yes.' His velvet drawl was more accented than was usual, but it still sent the same shivers up her spine. He took her arm and, turning it over between his fingers, ran his thumb along the blue-veined aspect of her wrist. Nell shivered; the fine invisible down on her skin stood on end. 'Your skin is like satin...'

A fractured sigh of shock escaped her parted lips. His eyes lifted to her face; the darkness held a raw, needy hunger. Her stomach muscles tensed with excitement.

'And so soft.' His sensuous whisper made the heat low in her belly spread...rapidly.

She dredged deep and discovered enough strength to pull her hand away. She rubbed it along her hip but dropped it abruptly when the action drew his attention to the soft, inviting curve of her thigh. 'How can you talk like that?' she snapped furiously. 'With your girlfriend standing over there?'

'Nell—' Raul was cut off. Too self-absorbed to notice the crackling tension, Roxie, her phone conversation completed, interposed her body between them. 'It was Tris,' she explained to Raul. 'I sent your love.' She laughed at his pained expression and turned to Nell, her body language as lavish as her curves.

'How would you like to come to the party with us?' she asked in the manner of someone offering a great treat.

Nell looked at the woman in horror. '*I wouldn't!*' she declared, too repelled by the proposal to be tactful. She could see from Roxie's expression that she had been expecting the 'nice little nanny-type person' to be grateful for this offer. 'I mean, it's terribly kind of you but I—'

Not one to take no for an answer, however, Roxie did not let the younger woman's abhorrence put her off.

'You'd be doing me an enormous favour,' she cajoled. 'I'd be so grateful and so would...' she paused, prolonging the dramatic tension like the true performer she was before delivering the punchline '...Tristram Nichols.'

'Who?' Nell asked with an abstracted frown. Clutching

her towel, she decided that nothing short of an act of God was going to keep her here another second.

'Tristram Nichols,' Roxie repeated, looking at Nell as if she were from another planet. 'He played Ben Lucas in *Tomorrow's People...*?'

'Oh, is he an actor?'

Roxie's jaw dropped.

'He specialised in your archetypal English upper-class twit,' Raul cut in smoothly. 'I'm not sure how much acting is involved.'

'Raul!' Roxie reproached. 'Tristram is a marvellous actor. The thing is he is, or rather *was*, engaged to Laura Hill. The bitch, not satisfied with dumping him, has moved in with his best friend. She told the press before Tristram.' Her eyes narrowed. 'She's turning up at this party tonight complete with her new love; that's so, *so* typical of her!' she fumed. 'And poor Tristram can't *possibly* go without a partner. Not when the press are going to be there in force, and not turning up would be letting Laura win...'

It was only towards the end of this explanation, which Nell had been half listening to, that she realised what Roxie was suggesting.

She shook her head. 'Me!'

Roxie smiled.

Nell did some even more fervent head-shaking. 'You're joking. Oh, no, *definitely* no!'

'But you'd be perfect, mysterious...nobody will know who you are. Nobody will be paying any attention to the awful Laura, they'll all be wondering who you are, and she'll be sick.' This prospect seemed to afford Roxie considerable delight.

The woman, Nell decided, was obviously mad. 'I don't want people looking at me.'

Roxie misunderstood. 'Oh, don't worry about that. Give

me half an hour and some make-up. Not that you…' she began as it dawned on her she might have given offence.

'I'm sure your friend can find a more suitable partner for this party than me,' Nell said drily. 'Being such a famous actor.'

'I'm sure he knows a good escort agency.'

Roxie flashed Raul a censorious frown. 'Not in the next half an hour he couldn't, Nell.'

'Well, why did he wait until now?'

'They only broke up this morning and the poor dear has had the press on his doorstep ever since.'

'*This morning…?* And he's going to a party tonight? Isn't that a bit fast for a broken heart to heal?'

'This isn't just any party and Tris is good at hiding his feelings…'

Raul took hold of Roxie's elbow and drew her to one side. His expression suggested he'd heard enough about Tristram. 'In Roxie's world a marriage that lasts six months is considered remarkable, Nell,' he remarked drily. 'Come on, Roxie, your *Tristram* will just have to take it on the chin like a man, or stay at home.'

Roxie looked at him as though he'd suggested burning books was a good idea. '*Stay at home?*' she parroted. 'Have you *any* idea what sort of photo opportunity this party will offer?'

'No, or I wouldn't have agreed to go with you,' he replied bluntly.

'Tristram's last two films have been flops and in this business you're only as good as your last box-office receipts. It's incredibly important at the moment he gets some positive press.'

Raul's expression softened. 'You really care for the rat, don't you?'

'Well, I was married to the man.'

'Married?'

Neither responded to Nell's startled exclamation.

'I know you want to help, Roxie, but there's just no way Nell here could carry this thing off.' He took hold of her narrow shoulders and turned her around to face Nell. 'Look at her,' he commanded.

'I'll do it,' Nell heard herself say.

'You angel!' Roxie exclaimed, clapping her hands with delight and grabbing Nell before she had a chance to change her mind.

The last thing Nell saw as she was shepherded out of the room was Raul's dark features set in a furious mask.

CHAPTER THIRTEEN

HAVING enrolled the help of a maid, Roxie set about transforming Nell with single-minded determination that made Nell's head spin. Having first explained that there was no time for debate and Nell would just have to trust her, she went through Nell's wardrobe.

Her decision-making process was effective but brutal. She cut down the choice by emptying the contents onto the floor and flinging every item she stigmatised 'hopeless' over her shoulder. From those items left—a very small pile—she had chosen the black dress that Nell was now wearing.

Nell had bought the little bias-cut number in a moment of weakness at last year's sales, but had not had an opportunity to wear it since.

And probably never would have if she hadn't volunteered herself for this stunt. The dress actually couldn't have been simpler. It skimmed her slender figure but still managed to hug the tight swell of her firm breasts and draw attention to the feminine sway of her hips. It was much shorter than anything she usually wore—so short that Nell was concerned that it would expose the lacy bits on the top of her nude-coloured hold-ups. She had expressed her concern to Roxie, who had looked at her and said, 'That would be a bad thing because…?'

How could you reason with someone like that?

Nell caught a glimpse of herself in a mirror as they hurried past.

Oh, God!

Raul was right; I can't do this. And more to the point I don't even want to! He just shouldn't have said I couldn't do, and then I wouldn't have got mad and I wouldn't be here about to make a total fool of myself. So basically it's all his fault, she concluded with flawless logic.

'It's far too short,' Nell complained, tugging fretfully at the hem.

Roxie laughed. 'The dress looks terrific; so do you and you know it,' she accused. 'You know, I'm glad I went with the natural look—your skin's so good it's a shame to cover it up and that colour really works on your lips. Subtle but sexy,' she decided, summing up the effect of her work. 'My only regret,' she admitted with a sigh, 'is that we didn't have time to straighten your hair.' Her glance rested on the soft waves that rested on Nell's shoulders.

Nell, who had always wanted a swishing curtain of river-straight hair, wished they had had too.

'Now let's get the male reaction from Raul.'

The suggestion increased the sick churning in Nell's stomach.

'Do we have to?' she asked in a small voice.

'Ready?' Roxie asked, then without waiting for Nell to respond she grabbed her arm and unceremonially yanked her into the library, where Raul had retreated to wait for them, with a flourish.

'Well?' she demanded. 'What do you think?'

Raul unhurriedly closed the laptop on the desk in front of him and raised his head. His dark eyes swept over Nell's slim figure.

'Very nice.'

The anticlimax was intense. All that anticipation was for what? *Serve you right,* she told herself, *for wanting to impress him.* If the rest of the male reaction she got was as tepid as that she received from Raul she might just as well be invisible.

'*Very nice?*' Roxie echoed, looking annoyed. 'She looks bloody marvellous and you know it,' she accused.

An enigmatic smile touched Raul's mouth. 'She is beautiful, so nothing has changed.' Without waiting for the two women to respond he shrugged his way back into his jacket. 'If we are going to this party, hadn't we better go before the photographers go home?'

Nell walked out to the waiting car in a daze. *He thinks I'm beautiful…?*

'You've got to be very nice to Nell, Tris, because you have no idea how difficult it was to persuade her to do this. Also she hasn't the faintest idea who you are. Get in the back seat and get to know one another,' Roxie told her ex-husband. 'Though not in the biblical sense,' she added laughingly.

In the rear-view mirror Nell caught sight of Raul's eyes. If it wasn't a trick of the light she put down the fury she briefly saw reflected in his those still dark depths to the fact he didn't like Roxie's ex-husband. Perhaps he found the fact that she openly admitted to still being fond of her ex difficult?

Tristram, who was blond and smoothly good-looking, turned out to be an undemanding sort of companion with a refreshingly dry sense of humour. If he was emotionally devastated he was hiding it well, but then maybe he was just very good at acting? Nell, who had been expecting to spend the evening propping up the bruised ego of some narcissistic actor, was pleasantly surprised.

While the conversation in the back seat became more animated and the laughter more frequent as the journey progressed, a heavy silence reigned in the front seat; even animated Roxie lost her sparkle.

The flash bulbs were popping before they even got out of the car. Nell blinked, blinded by the sea of lights. People were shouting Tristram's name and inundating him with questions; he smiled and waved, totally unfazed.

It was only when she stumbled that Tristram noticed how alarmed she was. He steadied her, smiled into her dazed face and tucked her hand in his.

'Don't worry, I'll take care of you.'

This caring comment earned him a murderous glare from Raul, who much to Roxie's visible frustration stalked past the phalanx of photographers without pausing and without once taking advantage of the photo opportunities.

'What's bitten him?' Tristram muttered, nodding his head towards Raul who, along with Roxie, had reached the relative sanctuary of the hotel, which had been taken over for the party to promote the latest blockbuster film, just in front of them. Nell assumed it was a historical drama because all the staff were dressed in eighteenth-century costume.

'I know he's got moody and broody off to a fine art, but even for him that was something else.'

Nell shrugged and accepted a glass of champagne from a boy in tight breeches. If she hadn't been so stressed she might even have been amused that Raul's antipathy was fully returned by the actor. The Roxie factor raising its head?

'Mind you, maybe I should try it—they do say treat 'em mean and keep 'em keen. It works for him. Did you see how the flash bulbs were after him?'

'I didn't see anything; I was blinded,' Nell confessed.

Tristram patted her hand and looked solicitous. 'I keep

forgetting you're not used to this. You did great, a little trouper. Have the drink, it'll make you feel better.'

Nell followed his advice and downed the drink. 'I was thirsty,' she explained.

'So I see.'

'Listen, if you have to...work the room, I'll be fine on my own.'

At her earnest words Tristram, whose attention had drifted towards his ex-wife, who was hanging on Raul's arm with an adoring expression, switched his focus back to Nell. He placed his hands on her shoulders.

'You're very sweet.'

A dissatisfied look settled on Nell's face. In her book 'sweet' was only a step away from 'homely'. 'I'd much prefer to be sexy,' she confessed wryly.

There was a moment's startled silence before Tristram threw back his head and laughed. The attractive warm bass boom drew a number of interested looks. When he had stopped laughing Tristram took Nell's chin in his hand and tilted her face up to him.

She had quite a long way to look. He was tall, but not as tall as Raul... *God! I've got to stop comparing every man I meet with Raul.*

'You are sexy,' he promised. '*Very* sexy. That hair is *incredible*,' he breathed, lightly brushing a burnished strand from her brow.

'And real, apparently,' observed a voice from behind him.

Nell couldn't be sure, but was Roxie's smile a little dimmer than earlier? Roxie placed a hand on her ex-husband's shoulder. 'Rafe Barrett is over there,' she told him, indicating the famous director with a nod of her head. 'He's still not cast the lead in his new film.'

'Later,' Tristram said. 'Right now I feel the urge to dance. Nell?' He held out his hand to Nell.

'I don't dance very well,' she warned him.

'But I do,' he replied as his fingers closed around hers.

Nell had not expected to enjoy the evening, but she did. Normally quiet at social occasions, preferring to watch and listen, she became quite animated. The champagne might have had something to do with it, or maybe the attentive company of a handsome man? Either way everything went swimmingly and she was being very witty and having a marvellous time until she emerged from the powder room and walked straight into Raul.

'Were you waiting for me?' she demanded—now that *was* the champagne. Under normal circumstances she would never have voiced her suspicions out loud.

'Just how much of that have you had?' he asked as she snatched a glass off the tray of a passing waiter.

'I haven't been counting.'

Raul examined her overbright defiant eyes and flushed cheeks. 'You are drunk,' he accused.

'I am not!' she gasped, outraged. 'And even if I was,' she added mutinously, 'it's got nothing whatever to do with you!'

Anger flared in his eyes. 'It has everything to do with me,' he said through gritted teeth. 'You are living under my roof.'

'But not sleeping in your bed,' she cut back loudly enough for several people close by to hear.

Raul, all too aware that several conversations around them dropped in volume as people strained to hear their argument, bit back his response. 'I'm taking you home.'

This announcement succeeded in breaking Nell's enraptured contemplation of the muscle that was clenching and unclenching in his lean brown cheek. She blinked up at him, then gave a scornful laugh.

'I don't think so, and I really don't see how you can make me,' she mused. 'What are you going to do, Raul, fling me over your shoulder kicking and screaming?'

His nostrils flared; their eyes clashed. 'Do not think I would not.'

Feeling an unfamiliar recklessness flow through her veins—or was that wine?—Nell let her eyes linger deliberately on the sensual contours of his mouth before she lifted her eyes to his. 'Dare you,' she challenged languidly.

Raul's hands clenched into fists at his side as he fought the impulse to call her bluff. 'You are making a fool of yourself,' he condemned finally between clenched teeth.'

Nell shrugged. 'My privilege,' she sniffed.

'Do not turn your back on me,' Raul said with gritted teeth.

Nell swung gracefully back, one hand on her hip, her head thrown back. 'Why, do you want to dance?' she mocked, lifting her eyes to his strained profile. She saw something move behind his eyes and knew that her recklessness had made her go too far. She placed her glass down on a table-top. 'You're right, I have had too much…'

'Yes,' he cut in.

She shook her head and looked confused.

'I will dance with you.' He laid a hand into the small of her back and drew her hard against him. 'Why should I be the only one not to?' he murmured grimly into her fragrant hair.

After the first few stumbling steps Raul felt the resistance leave her body. Her slim body moulded to him like a second skin as they flowed together. As one unit they moved, not to the slow beat of the music, but to the throb of desire that coursed through their veins. Her head was tucked under his chin; he could smell her hair and the perfume she was wearing. Through the thin fabric of her dress Raul could feel the heat of her skin.

He felt her gasp and sigh as he allowed her to feel his erection.

The punitive anger that had made him drag her onto the dance floor was leaving him, but the desire he felt was not. The control he prided himself on was slipping. He half closed his eyes and imagined sliding his hands under the skirt of that sexy little dress. He would run his fingers along the soft velvety skin on the inside of her thighs right up to… *Right here on the dance floor in front of everyone— nice move, Raul!*

He had to cool things down. She was drunk and he was insane.

Breathing hard, he pulled back slightly from her, but she immediately pressed herself against him, her supple curves slotting into his harder contours as if they were two halves of a whole.

Nell was dimly conscious of the music stopping. There was air between them and her brain started functioning again.

'I don't dance very well,' she heard herself say stupidly.

That hadn't been dancing, that had been…that had been the most mind-blowingly erotic experience of her life and probably could have got them arrested in any number of places!

She looked around, amazed that people weren't pointing and staring. Had they not realised what had been happening?

She looked up at Raul, saw the dark scores of colour high along his slanting cheekbones and the restive glitter in his heavy-lidded eyes. He had, she thought.

'You don't need to,' he replied cryptically before turning

on his heel and leaving her standing there in the middle of the dance floor feeling like an idiot.

'Are you all right?'

Nell smiled; Tristram had found her in her dark corner. He looked so normal and, more importantly, *she* could look at him and not feel like some sex-obsessed love slave.

'Not especially,' she admitted with a tight smile.

'Do you feel like getting out of here?' he asked impulsively.

'Out where to?'

'Wherever you like.'

They ended up in a small smoke-filled jazz club where Tristram spent the entire time talking about his ex-wife and Nell, who was getting soberer by the second, contemplated her behaviour at the party with growing horror.

Later in the taxi home Tristram recalled some amusing anecdote and surprise, surprise the main character in the amusing tale was Roxie.

'Most women would have been screaming their heads off,' he said. 'But not Roxie. Do you know what she did?'

'Why did you get divorced, Tristram? I mean, you're obviously still in love with her.'

Her companion began to hotly disclaim it, then caught Nell's eyes. He sighed. 'We were both busy with our careers and we just drifted apart.'

'Other people?'

'That is always a problem in our industry. You spend so long apart. So, all right,' he sighed, catching Nell's expression, 'that's no excuse. I guess it's true—you never appreciate what you have until it's gone,' he admitted.

'And now she's with Raul.'

'Yeah, it sort of looks that way,' he agreed gloomily.

Nell couldn't think of anything to say that would make

him feel better—not without lying. Tristram was charming, had a great sense of humour and liked women, but would any woman leave Raul for him? Nell didn't think so.

Feeling like a teenager who'd stayed out past her curfew, Nell crept furtively up the stairs with her shoes dangling in her fingers. She didn't go directly to her room; instead she looked in the children's rooms—both were dead to the world. The sleep of innocence, she thought with a tinge of envy.

Outside in the hallway Nell pressed her shoulders against the wall and heaved a sigh. There was an expression of poignant regret reflected on her face as she closed her eyes briefly and gathered her thoughts. She had wondered a lot over recent days how she would know when she should leave, but tonight the decision had been made for her.

This was where she wanted to be, but it wasn't where she belonged.

It would be best for everyone, including her. The children would miss her a little at first, but not for long; they had made new friends and a new life. She angrily blinked back the tears of self-pity that rose in her eyes and lifted her chin. She had fallen in love with Raul—but people suffered unrequited love every day of the week and survived.

So would she.

There were things that would be harder to survive, she reflected grimly, and if she stayed around here she'd experience them.

Her breathing quickened and her pupils dilated as she recalled the hunger stamped on Raul's hard, strongly etched features when he had looked at her. The memory of being held in his arms, feeling the erotic imprint of his hot, hard body was something she would never forget, but it was something she couldn't let happen again.

She knew that Raul was a sensual man, a man with strong appetites. A man used to seeing something he wanted and taking it—hell, wasn't that part of what turned her on about him? But it wasn't enough for her.

She wasn't naïve or judgmental—people had affairs, it happened—but it wasn't something she wanted for herself. If there hadn't been a Roxie she might have been prepared to compromise her principles—actually there was no 'might' about it. But Roxie was a fact, and one thing Nell couldn't compromise on was exclusivity. Neither would she be the other woman.

The problem was if Raul touched her, her high-flown principles would be history, and she knew it, which meant she had to make sure he never did, and fast!

People didn't really die of a broken heart, she told herself as she pushed open her bedroom door. She closed it behind her and leaned against it before reaching out for the dimmer switch.

'Where the hell have you been? Do you know what time it is? *Three-thirty*…' Raul intoned grimly without consulting the watch on his wrist.

The shock of finding him like a dark avenging angel standing there momentarily sent her brain into shut-down.

His dark eyes raked the slim body standing before him. 'Do you realise how inconsiderate this sort of behaviour is? Well?' he demanded, taking an impetuous step towards her frozen, wide-eyed figure.

The action jolted Nell to a weak response.

'What are you doing in my room? In the dark?'

Her hungry eyes swept over the hard contours of his hard, masculine body. Devastatingly beautiful—*always*—but no longer perfectly groomed. His tie and jacket were gone, and his shirt buttons undone to mid-waist—*Do not go there, Nell!* His normally sleek dark hair was standing up spikily. The image evoked two very strong but contradictory desires in Nell. She wanted to smooth back his hair and rip off his clothes.

Not necessarily in that order.

'Do you?'

Nell blinked.

'What sort of message are you sending Katerina with this kind of behaviour?' His mouth compressed in a thin, disapproving line as he visibly fought to contain his feelings.

'She's asleep,' Nell rebutted weakly. 'And I'll be up in time to take them to school.'

Eyes like black ice drilled into her. '*School…?*' he echoed contemptuously. 'This isn't about school!' he thundered.

'Then what is it about?' she asked quietly.

The question halted him quite literally in his tracks. Nell, who had never seen Raul, the master of the cutting one-liner, at a loss for words before, found it disorientating to see him struggle to express himself.

'Have you been waiting up for me?'

The quiet question earned her a glare of profound disbelief.

'Whatever gives you that idea?' He ran a savage hand through his disordered hair and took a deep breath. 'I spent an hour looking for you at that damned interminable party before some idiot mentioned he'd seen you go off with Nichols.' There was a rasping vibration in his forceful drawl as he lowered his eyelids abruptly over a look of seething fury. 'The least you could have done was let someone know you were leaving.'

'I don't see why. Do I have a curfew?'

'What you're supposed to have is self-respect,' he lashed contemptuously.

Nell's cheeks burned with angry mortification. 'You've got no right to speak to me that way. You're not responsible for me.'

'Well, someone needs to be because you're quite obviously not fit to look after yourself.'

In her turn Nell was becoming angry. 'At least I'm not a hypocrite.'

His eyes narrowed on her angry face. *'Meaning?'*

'Meaning,' she choked, 'when was the last time you spent the night in your own bed? And just for the record I've been looking after myself with reasonable success since I was eighteen,' she retorted, resentful of this incompetent female tag he had attached to her.

'Is that including the years you lived with my brother?'

'My life would have been very different if Javier hadn't been there for me,' she agreed quietly. 'He was a very special person.'

The anger abruptly drained from his face, leaving him looking very much like a man who'd spent a sleepless night. He ran a hand over his jaw where the heavy shadow looked bluish black. 'My father was never the same after he left,' he revealed unexpectedly. 'And I know that obeying Father and not contacting Javier was the hardest thing that Mother ever did.'

'I suppose they were glad they still had you…?'

She was disappointed but not surprised when Raul displayed no inclination to enlarge upon his previous comments; she had already noticed that he didn't like to talk about himself. He was very adroit at *not* answering personal questions. All part of his self-contained, self-controlled in-charge persona.

'Where have you been? I know you didn't go back to his flat.'

'How do you know that?'

'Because I went there,' he revealed in a driven tone.

'You did?' Nell stared at him. Had he taken Roxie with him on this save-Nell-from-herself expedition? 'Well, I wasn't there.' For a moment she contemplated the scene that might have occurred if she had gone back for coffee and Raul had arrived in this belligerent mood.

'I know that now,' he snarled 'But where else was I supposed to look?' he muttered thickly. 'You were drunk, and that sleaze is just the type to take advantage,' he pronounced before muttering something dark in Spanish.

Nell felt impelled to defend this slur on Tristram's good name.

'Tristram wouldn't do anything of the sort.'

Raul's jaw tightened aggressively; the bands of colour that were highlighting the strong masculine angles of his cheekbones had deepened several shades.

'But I would, I suppose.' And wouldn't she have some justification to think this? Wasn't the reason he didn't think Tristram could have spent the evening with her without making a move that he was sure as hell he couldn't have!

Nell looked startled by the abrupt accusation. 'I didn't say that. I know you don't like him because of Roxie,' she said, injecting an understanding note into her voice even though inside she felt like screaming, 'but Tristram is really a very nice man and he wouldn't do anything like that.'

'Unless you asked him to.'

There was a pulsating silence. An angry tear slid down her cheek. She brushed it carelessly away.

'Maybe I *wanted* to be taken advantage of,' she flung recklessly. 'But not by him.'

Raul inhaled, the sound loud in the room as his chest

expanded. Eyes dark as obsidian melded to Nell's scared iridescent blue gaze, he slowly exhaled. There was no discernible expression on his face to give her a clue to what he was feeling, but the tension in the room had zoomed off the scale in the past few seconds.

'We didn't...I didn't...we went to a club and talked...' *Why am I telling him this? Why did I have to say anything at all?*

Nell wanted the floor to open up and swallow her. She had as good as handed him an invitation and he hadn't responded. It was pretty difficult to interpret that as anything other than rejection, which was what happened when you were rash and foolish enough to reveal your innermost feelings. It was a blessing that her wayward tongue had stopped short of expressing her undying love!

The night is still young, Nell, the voice in her head contributed drily.

'A lot of talking.' His expressive upper lip curled contemptuously as, hands thrust deep into his pockets, he began to pace up and down in a tight circuit. 'No wonder Roxie left him.'

'I think it much more likely you're the reason she left him,' Nell retorted acidly.

Raul's eyes narrowed and his head reared. 'I do not sleep with married women.'

'Wow!' she gushed insincerely. 'That must really cramp your style. Actually, I'd have thought married women were *just* your style. Being as they're so much less likely to require anything approaching commitment, aren't they?'

There was a white line of fury etched around Raul's sensually sculpted lips. 'For the record, I met Roxie about two years after they split up; a lot of water had passed under the bridge in that time.'

'And men.' Under his ironic stare the apples of Nell's

cheeks turned a mortified pink. She deeply regretted the catty riposte the moment it left her lips, but her attempts to put things right emerged sounding pretty unconvincing even to her. 'I really like Roxie. I think she's a very honest person.'

'Sure,' he mocked. 'The warmth and sisterly sentiment just jumped out and hit me when you were calling her a tart. Perhaps you should try for a bit of that honesty yourself.'

'I wasn't calling her a tart,' Nell denied hotly. 'And, considering how you've been coming out with snide, slanderous comments about Tristram all night, I don't really think you've got any room to talk. I don't know why you're being so nasty about him. If anything had happened tonight it would have been me that was taking advantage; Tristram is obviously on the rebound.' And desperate to rebound back to his ex-wife.

'I've seen heartbroken and he wasn't it.'

'God, you're a callous bastard,' she accused. She took a deep breath; when you started name-calling it was time to call it a day. 'Look, this is going nowhere. I'm really sorry if you were concerned...or was it Roxie who was concerned?' If Roxie had had him running around looking for her traumatised ex all night that would explain his vile humour and obvious frustration.

'Roxie went on to a club,' he revealed shortly.

'Without you?'

'As I am standing here, obviously without me.' This hadn't pleased Roxie. In fact Roxie hadn't been pleased with him full stop tonight.

Raul had told Roxie a long time ago that there was just no spark. But Roxie had known that being seen as a couple would give her a lot of expensive publicity for free. Tonight she'd suggested that free publicity wasn't worth going around with someone who acted as if you were invisible.

'I'm sorry if you missed out because of me.'

'I was out of my mind with worry because of you,' he interrupted starkly.

'Well, that does seem a little excessive.'

'Excessive,' he repeated in a low, impassioned accent. *'Excessive?'* No longer low, his voice rose to a heavily accented bass bellow of outrage. 'Shall I show you excessive?'

CHAPTER FOURTEEN

In two steps Raul had reached Nell. It took another heart-beat for him to frame her face in his hands and seal his mouth to hers with a hungry force that sent her arching backwards.

When he eventually lifted his mouth from hers Nell's heart was hammering; she could feel the blood throbbing through her veins. Her senses were swimming. All thought of rejection had been blitzed from her mind the moment he had touched her. She wanted him, his possession, in every fibre, every cell of her body! The wanting left no room for any other thought in her head.

'Oh, God!' His dark features swam before her eyes. She blinked and tried to focus. 'That was perfect,' she cried, leaking self-control fast. '*You're* perfect.'

'This is going to be perfect,' he promised thickly.

'What is?'

Though his expression was fiercely needy, a glimmer of wry amusement flashed across his face. 'I think you know,' he suggested throatily.

Her eyes still welded to the strong lines of his amazing bronzed face, Nell gave a tiny nod of acknowledgement. 'I just wanted to hear you say it. I want to know if it sounds the way I imagined,' she revealed with a mixture of self-consciousness and defiance.

'I am going to take you to bed and make love to you.' His head lowered as he ran his thumb over the full curve of her full, pouting lower lip before catching the soft, sensitive flesh in his teeth and tugging gently. 'How does tha measure up to your fantasies?'

'I think I prefer the real thing,' she confided shakily.

'This real?' Taking her hand in his, he pulled it onto hi body.

Nell felt the hard ridge of his erection pulse against th constriction of his trousers. He grinned as her eyes widene in shock and then, with his eyes still fastened to hers, h slid his tongue inside her mouth. The skilful, sensual pen etration made her groan.

Nell shuddered as liquid warmth filled the lower half o her body. Her body went limp and his supporting arm tigh ened across her narrow ribcage.

Raul gave a gleaming smile of predatory satisfactior 'I've been wanting to do that for a long time,' he confesse throatily.

Nell found her back pressed against the wall without hav ing any recollection of how she had got there. The pleasur of his touch bordered on the intolerable. Could a perso overdose on bliss? Nell felt as if she were drowning in hi eyes.

She shuddered and said his name as he touche his tongue to the corner of her mouth. 'You're so…so.. mmm…' she breathed as his lips moved down the colum of her neck. His kisses were addictive. He was addictive Her fingers began to tug frantically at his belt.

Raul lifted his head, looked into her flushed, aroused fac and shining, adoring eyes.

'And you, my little one, are so beautiful, so desirable First the black swimsuit, then this dress…' He drew a deep ragged breath. 'I have been through several sorts of hel thinking of someone else doing what I wanted to…' H covered her hand with his and helped her unfasten his belt

The thought of Raul fantasising about making love t

her was more than her brain could cope with. 'And what else did you want to do?'

'Many things,' he told her in a voice that made her shiver helplessly with anticipation. 'But first…' His hand moved confidently to mould the swell of one breast.

Nell's eyes widened with incredulous wonder and then closed tight as a wave of deep pleasure vibrated through her body. Biting her lip as his fingers found the prominent bud of her nipple, she pressed her face into his shoulder and gave a sob of pleasure.

Raul's hand went to the back of her head, his fingers massaging her nape, pressing deep into her thick, silky hair. The fluid musical flow of deep, vibrant Spanish made no sense to Nell but it was the sweetest, most exciting sound she'd ever heard.

He reached a hand behind her and pulled down the zip of her dress; it slipped over her shoulders. Eyes like flames licked down the pale curves of her partially clothed body. 'Take it off, I want to see you,' he breathed thickly as he lowered his mouth to hers.

She stood there panting when he lifted his head.

Do you know what you're doing, Nell? She let her eyes meet his and the answer to the question no longer seemed relevant.

There was an air of defiance that Raul found oddly touching as she slid the dress off her shoulders. It fell and so did his gaze. She stood there in a black strapless bra, matching pants and stockings. The ache in his groin intensified to a painful degree.

'My God, you're beautiful.' There was an awed wonder in his raw observation.

Until he spoke Nell hadn't been aware that she had been holding her breath awaiting his reaction. As her body swayed towards him Raul grabbed the back of her head.

'You are driving me crazy.'

They kissed, one passionate kiss blending seamlessly into the next, no two alike, all perfect and totally mind-blowing. Raul took his kissing seriously. Nell drifted along on the crest of a wave of discovery and delight until she felt his hands slide along her inner thigh, skimming over the sensitive skin towards the top of her stockings.

Raul felt her body jerk and stopped. 'You don't like that?' he asked thickly.

She was finding it difficult to form words; her lips felt swollen and strange. She touched them with her tongue and saw the pupils of Raul's eyes dilate dramatically.

'I don't like you stopping.' The force of emotions stronger than anything she had ever imagined possible wrenched the husky confession from her.

Raul gave a laugh of startled delight. The laughter was still vibrating in his chest when he placed his hands around her narrow waist and lifted her to waist-height.

'Then I won't stop.'

Nell's legs automatically locked around him to seal their bodies at waist-level. An earthy groan was drawn from the depths of his chest as her arms went around his neck until her breasts were flattened against him.

As he walked backwards towards the bed Nell continued to press kisses to his face and neck. When the back of his knees touched the bed Raul sat down slowly, taking Nell with him.

Nell blinked to find herself sitting on top of him. She ran her fingers down his throat; his golden skin was covered with a faint sheen of sweat. She tasted the salty tang of it when she touched her tongue to the pulse-point that throbbed at the base of his neck.

She laid her open-palmed hand on his chest then, with a

ltry smile, straightened her elbow. The pressure sent Raul ackwards onto the bed.

His deep, throaty laugh sent shivers of desire down her ine.

She made the most gloriously primitive sight. A red-aired beauty astride him, an elemental figure, she was the ost incredibly erotic thing he had ever seen in his life.

'I'm all yours.'

Having control placed firmly in her court, Nell experi-ced a brief flurry of panic—she didn't know what to do ith it! Seconds later a latent sensuality in her make-up at she hadn't known was there kicked in and took control.

Eyes half shut, Nell leaned forward, her body loose and pple. The action caused her hair to brush lightly against aul's face as she planted her hands either side of his head.

In response to Raul's slow fingertip exploration of the nooth flesh of her shoulders her head went back, exposing e long, lovely line of her white throat.

It wasn't until she registered the touch of cool air on her in that she realised he had unfastened her bra.

Raul, unable to resist the temptation of the sway of her nk-tipped, unfettered breasts, took the weight of one soft ound in the palm and, drawing it towards him, fastened s teeth around one delicious tight bud.

'Oh, God, Raul!' she gasped and squirmed against him his tongue began to stroke and tease her sensitised flesh. he managed to endure the sweet torture for a matter of conds before the strength went out of her arms and she ollapsed on him in a soft, panting heap.

Raul slid his fingers deep into her hair, ran his tongue ver the pulse at the base of her throat, and tipped her over to her side. Nell, finding her hands free, grabbed his head d plunged her tongue into his mouth. She felt a shocked

quiver run through his lean frame before he began to kiss
her back, matching and surpassing her raw hunger.

The fractured words of husky Spanish that fell from his
lips when they weren't pressed to hers sent her deeper into
the spiral of passion.

'Yes,' he murmured in throaty approval as her hands began to rip frantically at his clothes.

His shirt parted under her determined assault, and with
a sigh of relief she spread her fingers across the warm,
slightly damp skin of his chest, twisting her fingers into the
whorls of dark body hair scattered across his lean, rippling
torso.

Raul lay there with his eyes closed, breathing hard as
she pulled back and her fingers skated across the flat ex-
panse of his washboard-hard belly. She watched with fascination the visible contraction of taut muscle under her
fingers.

'You're perfect.' At her dazed whisper his eyes opened.

'You want me?' he breathed, removing himself from her
to slide his buttonless shirt from his shoulders.

Mutely she nodded.

Satisfaction male and primitive flared in his eyes as he
slid his trousers over his lean hips and kicked them aside,
his boxers swiftly followed suit—not that they had con-
cealed much from her fascinated gaze to begin with. His
body was a perfect blend of power and grace. Her throat
ached and the fist of desire that clutched low in her belly
tightened as she looked at him with helpless longing.

'Now,' he announced, 'it's my turn.'

Nell closed her eyes as she felt his hands mould her
aching breasts, weigh them in his hands, tease the already
engorged peaks before moving over her stomach, skimming
over the gentle mound of her belly, before sliding lower

his fingers peeling the tiny briefs back, and sliding them down her legs.

Her breath came in tiny gasps as he kissed the arch of her foot before touching the soft red-gold fuzz at the apex of her legs. His exploration deepened and her body arched, but she settled back and opened her legs in mute invitation.

It was an invitation he accepted without hesitation. His slow, sensual exploration drove her to the brink of release several times. By the time he settled between her thighs she was sobbing his name.

She gasped as she felt the touch of his velvet hardness and a keening cry left her lips as he thrust deep into her. The sensation of being filled was incredible. Better than anything she had dreamed possible. She was vaguely conscious of shouting something along these lines as he remained strangely immobile suspended above her, but part of her.

Her vocal semi-articulate appreciation continued as he began to move deep and slow within her, feeding the raw urgency in her blood, until she felt she could bear it no longer. Just as she felt the first quivers of an orgasm that began in the deepest part of her and spread out to involve every part of her body he cried out her name and slammed hard into her twice.

She felt the warmth of his release as her entire body was bathed in the golden glow of completion. She stroked his slick golden back as he lay spent on top of her.

It was a little while later, when his breathing had slowed, that he slid off her. He lay on his back looking at the ceiling, not touching her.

That bothered her.

'You didn't sleep with Javier?'

His words gave her a sinking feeling. 'Javier never

wanted to sleep with me.' It didn't even occur to Nell that she had to say she had never wanted to sleep with Javier.

The hand she had been about to place on his shoulder froze mid-air as her eyes met his furious gaze. 'You are drunk…'

'No, I'm not.'

'*Drunk!* I slept with a drunk virgin. A drunk virgin who was thinking about my brother!'

'*I wasn't!*'

Ignoring her bewildered denial, he leapt from the bed in one fluid motion and began to pull on his clothes with haphazard haste. 'I have to go,' he said, avoiding her eyes.

'Stay. We need to talk.'

His hot gaze roamed over her pale body. 'If I stay, we won't talk, and I've no intention of making a bad decision worse by repeating it.'

Bad decision!

She cried for a while after he had gone and then, when she was all cried out, she sat up. With a decisive sniff she straightened her shoulders and blew her nose.

She knew what she had to do.

CHAPTER FIFTEEN

'WELL, Miss Rose, everything's fine. As you saw on the scan you have a healthy baby and your dates are bang on—you are twelve weeks almost exactly.'

Nell, who had been preparing herself for the worst, gave a sigh of relief. 'But the bleeding…?' she began anxiously.

'A small blood loss is not unusual about the time your period would have been due in the early weeks while your body is adjusting to hormone levels.'

'Then I can go home?'

'You can.' The doctor looked at her over the top of his half-moon spectacles. 'Remember to take things easy, no dashing around, and if you have *any* worries go straight to your GP.'

'I will,' Nell promised.

Nell passed through the maternity and antenatal departments. Seeing pregnant women *en masse*, some in the final stages of pregnancy and absolutely vast, reminded Nell of how her own body was already changing.

Will I ever be that big?

Her eyes fixed on her still-flat waistline, she promptly blundered into a nurse who was preceding a very pregnant woman through a doorway. The woman in the flowery smock was walking with her arm linked through that of a man. You didn't have to ask for a blood test to know that he was the father…he positively glowed with pride.

Nell smiled as he held the woman's elbow as she lowered herself awkwardly into a chair; he acted as though she were made of glass. *That's the way it's supposed to be,* she thought, *sharing all the…* Her smile faded and she turned quickly away.

I will never have that. I won't have someone to share this with me.

The wave of loss that swept over her was shocking in its intensity. She hurried out of the building and outside took several deep breaths of fresh air before setting off for home.

It was actually not so difficult for Nell to block out the memory of that happy couple; she had plenty of other things to occupy her thoughts. Now that the baby's survival was no longer occupying her thoughts to the exclusion of everything else, the old burning issue resurfaced.

What was the best way to tell Raul that their one night together had resulted in a baby in such a way that made it clear she wasn't asking for anything from him?

Of course it would be easier not to tell him at all. She had even tried to tell herself that it would be better for everyone if she kept him in ignorance, but she had always known deep down that this option was a non-starter.

Fathers, even accidental fathers, had rights, so, even though she didn't expect Raul to be happy about it, he did have the right to know that he had a child. One day the baby would want to know who his or her father was. At least if she was asked she could honestly tell her son or daughter that she had loved their father very much—this was a love-child in the truest sense of the word.

On the way home she stopped off at the supermarket to buy a few groceries. Coming out with her awkward carrier bags she didn't see the woman in the back of a black car who was staring at her.

Later that same night she finally completed the letter she had begun and abandoned so many times before. Sticking a stamp on it, she walked down to the post office, not trus

g herself to still be of the same mind in the morning. It
as growing dark by the time she retraced her steps to the
edsit she had rented.

She decided to take the long way back, because it was
etter lit, but even so when she heard the footsteps behind
er on the rainy pavement she quickened her pace. The
ootsteps did too. She slowed down and so did the foot-
eps.

Nell's heart thudded as fear raced through her veins. She
ooked around the street. It was deserted. She took a deep
reath and broke into a run. The adrenaline surging through
er bloodstream gave her feet wings. The door to her build-
g was only a hundred metres or so away.

Her goal was literally a couple of steps away when her
eel caught in a crack in the pavement and she lost her
ooting and fell heavily, landing on her hands and knees.
ain jarred through her, robbing her momentarily of the
ower of speech.

Two strong hands beneath her arms began to haul her
p and she totally lost it. Convinced that she was about to
ecome the victim of some violent stalker, she stamped
own with all her might on her attacker's instep while at
e same time jabbing viciously backwards with her elbow.

Both blows connected and Nell gave a grim smile as she
eard him grunt in pain. His grip loosened and Nell took
er opportunity and tore free. As she did so she half turned
ack, her red-gold hair whipping around her face as she
ced her attacker, her fists clenched.

Shock froze her to the spot, the battle light fading from
er eyes. *'You?'* she breathed. Her wide gaze clung help-
ssly to the tall, greyhound-lean, dark-haired figure who
as straightening his jacket.

'Are you mad?' Raul demanded.

'I thought...I thought you were chasing me,' she faltered.

He released a low, frustrated hiss. 'Of course I was chasing; you took off as if...'

'As if someone was following me?' she suggested quietly.

'You thought I was...' Enlightenment softened the hard edges of his face. His eyes dropped to the hands still clenched into fists at her side. 'And what were you going to do?' he asked. 'Fight?'

His amusement brought a self-conscious flush to her pale cheeks. 'Well, I wasn't going to make it easy for him.'

A light of admiration entered Raul's dark eyes. He was still so angry that he couldn't look at her without wanting to demand how she could have walked out on him after that night they had shared.

The irony of this dramatic reversal of roles had not passed him by. He was the one who didn't stay the night with women because he didn't want them to get the wrong idea.

'Even your worst enemy would have to admit you have guts.'

'Is that what you are?' she asked warily.

'Are you hurt?'

Seeing him had driven everything else from her head, including the fact that her knees were grazed and bleeding. A quick glance convinced her the damage was superficial. She turned her hands palm up and brushed some of the loose gravel that had embedded itself in the soft skin away.

'A bit bruised but I'll...' Midway through dismissing his concern, she recalled the other life she was meant to be protecting. A wave of self-condemnation and mind-numbing fear swept over her.

Raul saw the colour leech from her skin just before she bent forward clutching her stomach.

He slipped a supportive arm across her back. 'What is it?' She gave no answer, just a low moan. 'Are you hurt? Is that it?' he demanded urgently.

Nell lifted her head and fixed her haunted eyes on his face. 'It's not me,' she denied, with an impatient shake of her head.

'Then what is it?'

'What if I hurt the baby when I fell?'

'The baby. What baby…?'

'Our baby.'

For several seconds he did nothing at all, just stood, an expression of blank incomprehension on his dark, gorgeous features. 'Y…you're saying…?'His eyes dropped to her belly; he swallowed. 'You're…?'

She nodded, appreciating his shock. She'd been pretty shocked herself when she had discovered their night of passion had resulted in her being pregnant, but she'd had time to grow accustomed to the idea.

'I'm pregnant. I'm sorry,' she added, because she felt manners required a show of contrition, though actually she didn't feel at all sorry. Scared sometimes, and worried about practical things such as how she would cope when the baby came—would she be a good mother? And was childbirth *really* as painful as they said? But that wasn't the same thing as sorry.

'God, I've only just come from the hospital. Do you think I should go back, Raul?'

'Hospital…baby… *Oh, my God!*' He closed his eyes.

Under the street lamp he looked ashen. He was taking it even worse than she had thought he would.

'Look, I only live up there.' Her backhanded gesture indicated the general direction of her flat. 'Do you think you can make it?' she asked gently.

Raul's eyes flickered open and he looked down at her anxious upturned features with an expression of blank incomprehension. 'What are you talking about? I am capable of walking a few steps.'

'Well, you didn't look it,' she revealed candidly. 'God, I'm really sorry I blurted it out like that,' she told him regretfully. 'But I guess I panicked. It would have been much easier in a letter…that's what I was doing,' she revealed. 'Posting a letter to you.'

'Your consideration for my feelings is profoundly moving.'

His sarcasm made her wince.

'However, I'm sure it is *easier* to fire a shot at someone from half a mile away using a telescopic sight than it would be to look them in the eyes and pull the trigger, but not necessarily for the person on the receiving end of the bullet!'

He'd prefer to be shot than have a baby, Nell interpreted unhappily.

'What are you doing?'

'I am taking you to the hospital,' he said, hefting her a little more comfortably into his arms.

'That really isn't necessary. The carrying or the hospital.'

'Shall we allow a properly qualified person to decide?' he suggested.

'I panicked,' she said in a small voice. 'I'd prefer to go home.'

'*Your* preferences are not a priority at present.' This blighting announcement reduced Nell to silence. A silence that lasted all the way to the hospital.

She looked at the tall building he pulled the car up in front of. 'This isn't my hospital.'

'It is now,' he snapped, picking her up as though she
ere a contagious disease.

Only in her most impracticable dreams had Nell allowed
erself to imagine him being tenderly concerned for her
ealth and delighted by the news he was to be a father.
ealistically she had anticipated his shock and even anger.
Vhat she hadn't allowed for was the hostility that seemed
• be directed at her. It wasn't as if she had got pregnant
• spite him and she had certainly not done it on her own!
Perhaps it was time to remind him of that…?

'Listen, you can't make me…'

Her feisty rebuttal died a death as dark eyes fastened
nto her face. 'I think you'll find I can make you do a lot
f things one way or the other, but we can discuss that
nce we have had the baby checked.'

'Am I supposed to believe you care?'

He inhaled sharply. 'My concern for the baby is the only
ing that is stopping me strangling you,' he revealed with-
ut inflection before turning to the receptionist and an-
ouncing he needed to see a doctor, and not any doctor—
aul knew exactly whom he wanted to see.

Having seen him in action, Nell was not surprised to find
erself being attended to by a blond medic who introduced
imself as Will James and immediately endeared himself
• Nell by asking her if she wanted Raul to stay while he
xamined her.

'Definitely not,' she said, beaming with gratitude to fi-
ally be given a say.

Raul was inclined to protest his exclusion. 'Really, Will,
at's not necessary.'

'The lady is the boss.' Smiling but firm, the doctor
aited until an impatient-looking Raul had left the room.
'Now tell me what is troubling you.'

'I've been and done this once today.' She sighed.

The doctor looked alert. 'Tell me about it,' he suggeste

'You know Raul?' Nell queried.

'Is that a problem?'

'It could be,' she admitted.

'I do know Raul, but I can assure you that our friendsh
doesn't alter the fact that anything you say to me will re
main confidential.'

'You know Raul and you can say that?'

The doctor laughed. 'I didn't say it would be easy.'

After the doctor left a cup of tea and biscuits appeare
About two minutes later again so did a nurse, asking if Ne
would like to see Mr Carreras. She looked relieved whe
Nell gave a nod of assent. Clearly she wasn't the only on
who found it hard to say no to Raul.

Seconds later an irate-looking Raul, his tie askew, h
normally sleek hair standing in spiky tufts around his hea
exploded into the room. He looked at Nell propped up con
fortably in bed drinking tea and his scowl deepened.

'Nobody has offered me tea,' he said, sounding more lil
a thwarted schoolboy than a dangerous playboy.

'I could ask for a second cup.'

'I don't want tea,' he retorted belligerently. 'The peop
here have been unhelpful and obstructive,' he announce
in a voice clearly pitched to travel beyond the confines o
her room. 'Nobody will tell me a thing!' he revealed in
throbbing voice of frustration.

'I expect they think it's none of your business.'

'None of my business!' he bellowed. '*Dios*...I'm the fa
ther.'

'You could always ask me.'

Her soft voice seemed to have a benign effect on hir
'I could,' he agreed.

'Have a seat, Raul,' she suggested.

Suspicion hardened the perfect lines of his proud face. 'Why, is it bad news?'

'No, not bad news,' she hastened to reassure him.

His shoulders visibly slumped in relief as, to her dismay, instead of taking the chair as she had expected he would he came to sit beside her on the edge of the bed.

Her nostrils twitched and her belly tightened as she greedily breathed in the male, Raul scent of him.

'So what did Will say?'

'That I'm pregnant.'

'You could have told me that…oh, I forgot, you favour the letter-writing option.' Raul closed his eyes and hissed something that sounded angry to himself in Spanish before opening them again. 'I'm sorry.'

'Me too,' Nell admitted. 'The letter thing was stupid. I take it you weren't in the street by accident when I walked by.'

He shook his head. 'Roxie saw you coming out a supermarket nearby earlier.'

'Oh, Roxie.' She gave a wooden smile. 'Is she well?' she asked, determined to be civilised about this.

She had been a passing fancy; Roxie was the woman he actually loved. The fact Raul had spent one night with her didn't give her any special rights—in fact it didn't give her any rights full stop.

Raul flashed her an impatient look. 'Yes, she's well.' And also, he suspected, not very happy with him. They had been about to sit down for lunch with a group of friends when she had mentioned that she had seen Nell earlier. She had not liked him dragging every last detail from her. She had liked even less him walking out just as the friends in question had been arriving—it was not cool to be sitting alone!

'I asked around the immediate area, but although several

people recognised your description nobody knew whe
you lived. So I waited.'

Her eyes widened. 'You *waited*?' This seemed an e
traordinary thing for him to do.

He nodded. 'It appears it is just as well I did. Fallin
like that could have had very serious consequences.'

Raul appeared to have forgotten that she wouldn't hav
fallen at all if he hadn't been there, but he looked so ol
viously shaken by the evening's revelations that she didn
have the heart to point this out.

'How pregnant are you?' She saw his eyes drop to h
lap as though he expected to see physical evidence of h
condition.

'Can't you figure that out for yourself?' She couldn
totally eliminate the bitterness from her voice. The date th
was etched in her memory obviously did not stand out .
anything significant in his social calendar.

'Twelve weeks.'

Her startled eyes lifted to his face and were held tig
by his compelling silver-flecked gaze. 'It's hardly likely
would have forgotten something I have regretted every da
since.'

His harsh admission was like a slap in the face. Nell
lashes came down to hide her hurt. She had hoped that tin
might have softened his attitude. *He must regret it eve
more now with a baby he doesn't want on the way,* sl
thought dully. She had to make sure he knew that as far
she was concerned he didn't owe her anything.

'Why did you leave that way? Without a word to an
one.'

The driven intensity in his deep voice brought her frow
ing attention back to his face. 'Because, like you said,' sl
began, choosing her words with great care, 'it was a mi
take, and one I didn't want to repeat either.'

Raul, desperately pale beneath his natural olive colouring, sucked in his breath through his flared nostrils. 'You think I would have forced myself upon you?' he demanded, outrage quivering in every power-packed inch of his lean body.

As her eyes slid greedily down his spare frame, despite the fact the circumstances were hardly conducive to such things she experienced an almost paralysing stab of lustful longing.

'No, of course not!' Nell rebutted as she dragged her eyes clear. She released a tiny self-derisory sigh. 'But I thought I might ask you to,' she admitted.

Nell squirmed in the heavy silence that followed her rash revelation.

So much for keeping things on a need-to-know basis— as in him not needing to know that I love him. Well, if I carry on coming out with gems like that there's not much chance of that.

'We both needed time out for things to cool down.' A century wouldn't cool her feelings. 'I thought it was for the best.'

'And what I thought was of no matter?' The dangerous edge in his silky enquiry was unmistakable.

'I knew what you thought,' she said flatly.

'Oh, I doubt that.' He released a sudden deep groan and Nell, who automatically looked up, found her face framed between a big pair of strong brown hands. His eyes scanned her face with a hungry ferocity. He swallowed hard before launching into a low, impassioned speech.

'You have to put the past behind you, Nell. Now more than ever with this baby coming.' She opened her mouth and he gave a low laugh. 'Oh, I *know* you think what you felt for Javier was love, but it wasn't. It was just a childish infatuation for a man far too old to be what you wanted. It

is understandable, you had lost your parents, you wer
looking for a father-figure more than a lover.'

She blinked at this erroneous reading of her relationshi
with Javier. 'That's not—'

He cut off her protest with an imperative shake of hi
head. 'I know it is hard for you to accept this, but yo
must. You've got to stop thinking it is betraying his mem
ory to have physical feelings for another man…for me,' h
added thickly. 'Because I know you do…Javier might hav
been your dream lover but you are a woman; dreams ar
not enough. You need a man of flesh and blood. A ma
who can hold you in his arms. *You need me!*' Dark eye
dared her to deny it.

Nell stared dumbly up at him, unable to understand wha
she was hearing in his voice, what she was seeing in hi
face.

'I had assumed you were lovers, and I was jealous a
hell. It made me ashamed to be jealous of my own brothe
and irrationally I turned my anger on you. I blamed yo
Dios!' he groaned, releasing her and sitting down on th
edge of the bed, his face buried in his hands.

He still thought she had been in love with Javier. Ho
could anyone so clever get it so wrong?

For a moment Nell just sat there watching the faint vi
brations that intermittently attacked his lean body. She wa
totally stunned by the storm of white-hot emotion that ha
spilled from him. She felt utterly and totally out of he
depth; her brain had gone blank trying to sift and mak
sense of so much information.

One thing she did know was that Raul was hurting an
that she couldn't bear. The instinct to offer him comfo
overrode everything else. She got to her knees and, pressin
her slim body to his back, curled her arms around him. Hi
hard body was warm through the thin hospital gown sh

had donned before her examination. She felt him tense, then as she laid her face against his shoulder heard a sigh whisper through his body.

After that neither of them spoke for some time.

It was Nell who finally broke the silence.

'Jealous…?'

Raul twisted and Nell found herself drawn onto his lap. She examined his well-loved features minutely. Raul's face was still drawn, but she thought he seemed calmer and more in control; or she did until their eyes locked. There was nothing calm about the fiery expression in his blazing eyes.

'Was it not obvious?' he demanded.

'Not to me,' she whispered. Could this entire situation ironically be the result of sibling rivalry? One brother wanted what the other had.

'You must marry me, of course.' There was something of his old autocratic manner in this decree.

Nell smiled sadly. 'I can't do that.' She might not be able to marry him, but she couldn't resist stroking his cheek.

'You are thinking that I might drop dead any moment?'

Nell gasped and her hand fell away. Eyes sparkling with anger, she pressed a hand to his lips. 'Don't talk about it.'

He removed her fingers and kissed each one in turn. By the time he had completed his task Nell's breath was coming fast and uneven, the room was spinning.

'I have had the tests. I got the results last week and I was given the all-clear. I have a future.'

But not with me.

Tears squeezed from underneath her tightly closed eyelids as she wrapped her arms tight about his neck and wept into his shoulder, unable to repress her relief.

'So, you see, there is no reason we should not marry.'

Nell lifted her tear-stained face. 'You don't want to get married; you said so.'

'I have changed my mind. Would you condemn a man because of a few foolish things he said in the past?' His compelling eyes raked her face angrily.

'It wasn't very long in the past,' she pointed out. 'People don't get married these days just because a baby is coming.'

'I am not interested in what *people* do,' he announced scornfully. 'I intend to be a full-time father to my child.'

If he had expressed such commitment to the idea of being her full-time lover she would have been over the moon. 'I'm sure we can arrange for you to be fully involved and I'm glad, of course I am,' she added huskily, 'that you have been given a clean bill of health.'

She gave a loud sniff. 'Not that that would make any difference. If you love a man it really doesn't matter if he is going to live fifty years or a week,' she explained wistfully.

He gazed at her with an expression of angry frustration. 'I am the father of your child; you will marry me if I have to drag you to the altar.'

'What about Roxie?'

His brows drew together in a puzzled line. 'What has she to do with us?'

'Everything, Raul.' Raul wanted her now, but he was a highly sexed man with strong appetites and no feelings of love to bind him to her. It was a need to compete with his elder brother that had driven him into her bed—that wouldn't keep him there.

'I'm afraid I don't share your attitude to sex, and I never will. When I get married I'm not going to develop a selective blindness about who my husband is sleeping with. Marriage has to be based on mutual love and respect to stand a cat's chance in hell of working!'

Raul's expression acquired a rock-like quality as he heard her out in silence.

'I think we have established that you do not love or respect me, and after the way I took advantage of you and didn't even have the sense to protect you I am not surprised. But the fact remains that I am the father of your child…and if you are able to let go of the past—'

'I don't want to let go of the past!' she interrupted fiercely. 'It holds memories that I will cherish for ever. And I do respect you, Raul, I do…love you. So much it hurts.'

'Incidentally, if you had picked up a newspaper in the last month you would know that Roxie and Tristram are to remarry next month.' He suddenly froze and rose jerkily to his feet, sending Nell sliding off his knee in a tangle of limbs.

'Oh, Raul, I'm so sorry about Roxie!' Nell said, finding her feet.

'*You love me…?*' Though barely audible, his incredulous words seemed to echo around the room.

Nell looked into his stunned face and blushed vividly. 'I didn't mean that precisely.'

'Well, you said that. *Precisely* that,' he added, a touch of complacence entering his deep voice.

'All right, then,' Nell conceded crossly. 'But I didn't know what I was saying.'

'Because you find it difficult to think straight when I am around…?' he suggested smoothly.

'I could hit you!' she declared, appalled by this display of callous self-satisfaction.

'Come here and kiss me instead.'

His bold eyes invited her, and Nell felt the familiar prickle of heat under her skin. She backed away, not trusting herself. 'Roxie,' she said, using the actress's name like a talisman to stop herself doing something really silly.

'I have had lovers in the past, but Roxie isn't one of them.'

Nell's jaw dropped. 'But you said…I thought…'

'I could see what you thought; it is hard not to when you walk around with your feelings written in neon across your forehead.' This recognition of her transparent vulnerability seemed to make him inordinately angry. 'It was not an assumption I did anything to dispel, admittedly. I was suffering agonies of jealousy so I didn't see why you shouldn't suffer just a little too.'

'You slept with me because of some sort of sibling rivalry. You didn't have to, you know; I never loved Javier… Well, I did, but I was never *in love* with him. He was almost like a father-figure to me.'

A hoarse laugh was wrenched from him. 'And you have the cheek to call *me* stupid! I slept with you, *querida*, because I couldn't *not*.'

Eyes as big as saucers blinked up at him.

'I was obsessed with you from the first moment I saw you,' he confided thickly. 'I convinced myself for a little while that I had brought you to live with us for the sake of the children, but in reality I brought you there because I couldn't bear to have you out of my sight. I still can't,' he revealed shakily.

'The last few weeks have been a nightmare. I couldn't even come after you at first, not knowing if I had a life to ask you to share with me, and when I knew I had you seemed to have vanished off the face of the earth. When Roxie said she'd seen you I could have kissed her.'

'But you didn't…?'

A smile glimmered in his deep-set eyes as he shook his head. 'I was in too much of a hurry.'

'Good. I don't think I like it when you kiss other women.

Kissing me is all right,' she added pointedly when he didn't move.

He moved fast enough then to satisfy even her impatience. His mouth closed over hers with a hunger that drove the breath from her body and the thoughts from her head. Nell responded with eagerness to the unashamed hunger of the hard male body she was pressed against. For several minutes they kissed with feverish passion as if they could wipe out the memory of the past few weeks' unhappiness from their minds.

'You will never leave me again,' Raul rasped huskily when they broke apart panting.

Nell gave a rapturous smile. 'I didn't want to leave you this time, only I didn't think you wanted me and I was so embarrassed at what I'd done.'

'You were so beautiful…so generous…so *wild*…' He broke off, laughing, and ducked the swing she took at him.

'Well, you didn't seem to mind too much at the time,' she recalled, flushing prettily at the memory.

His dark eyes sparkled wickedly. 'I thought I had died and gone to heaven. You were my every fantasy made real.' His voice dropped to a throaty whisper. 'You are my every fantasy.' He gave a frustrated groan and put her from him. 'Oh, God, if only you were not in this place!'

'Well, I don't actually have to be. The doctor did say I could go home any time I like. You're not the only one who got a clean bill of health,' she told him.

It took Raul several seconds to absorb what she had said. 'Then we don't have to be here?' he queried cautiously.

Nell shook her head. 'Nope.'

'*Dios!*' he exclaimed. 'Then why the hell didn't you say so before, woman?' he growled.

'What's the hurry and what about my tea?' she protested

as he grabbed her hand and her coat, which was hanging on a hook on the door.

'It's cold and the hurry is I am inhibited by this place.'

'And my clothes...Raul!' she protested laughingly.

'I'll buy you clothes,' he promised, sweeping her up into his arms.

'You think you can buy me?' she teased as he swept purposefully down the hospital corridor oblivious to the stares and comments they were attracting.

'I thought I could buy anything until I met you,' he corrected. 'But I have discovered that you cannot put a price on the important things in life and you, my love, are the most important thing in my life and always will be.'

Nell's eyes filled with emotional tears.

'You are crying?'

'I'm so h...happy,' she hiccuped.

'*Women*,' Raul said indulgently as he carried away his prize.

CHAPTER SIXTEEN

ON THEIR first anniversary Nell presented Raul with a portrait in oils she had done of him. Rather shyly she awaited his response; when he just continued to stare at it she couldn't resist prompting him.

'I think I caught your expression...?' she suggested. Then, when he still failed to respond, she gave a snort of exasperation. 'Well, do you like it?'

Raul lifted his head slowly. There was a dazed expression in his eyes.

'That is how you see me?' he asked wonderingly.

She nodded.

He swallowed. '*Querida*, you have an amazing talent. I will treasure this for ever.'

Nell blushed with pleasure. 'I think it helps to be in love with your subject matter.'

'I feel my own present will seem shamefully inadequate after this. I was going to get you that necklace you were drooling over when we were in Madrid last month, but I thought of something else. It is not here.'

'This is very mysterious,' she complained, watching him get little Javier into the cute little blue all-in-one bunny suit with the fur-lined hood. 'Won't you give me a hint?'

Raul shook his head and gave an infuriatingly enigmatic smile as he handed her the baby, who looked up at her with eyes very like his father. He was such a miracle that even after three months she still got choked up sometimes just looking at him. She knew that Raul shared her wonder; he was determined to be a hands-on dad and had cut back significantly on his workload since Javier had been born, to spend more time with his new family.

Sometimes she couldn't believe how lucky she was. The past year had been the happiest of her life.

'I think your daddy is very mean, don't you, Javier?' she complained to their son sleeping in the back of the car as Raul drove through the city. She received a gentle baby snore in reply.

'There's no good nagging or fluttering your eyelashes at me—I'm not telling you where we're going,' Raul told her sternly.

About ten minutes later, when they had reached an area she was not familiar with, Raul brought the car to a halt in front of a building site. 'Right, put this on.'

Nell stared at the bright yellow hard hat he had handed her. She looked quizzically up at her handsome husband. 'You've bought me a hard hat for our anniversary?'

'Just put it on, Nell,' he said, fitting one similar to the one he'd handed her over his own dark glossy hair.

'On him it looks sexy, on me...' Her complaint became a delighted laugh as she slid out of the car and saw Raul standing there with Javier in his arms; the baby had a miniature hard hat covering his fine silky baby curls. 'Oh, he looks so cute!' she exclaimed.

Raul adopted a hurt expression. 'And me, don't I look cute?'

'You're impossible,' she claimed.

He gave a wicked and wildly sexy grin that never failed to make her heart beat faster and stood to one side to let her pass him. 'Be careful, it's pretty uneven.'

After they'd walked fifty yards or so it still looked like a building site to Nell. There were hunky men in hard hats and checked jeans, scaffolding and dumper trucks—yep, a building site.

'You've bought me a building site?'

'Not exactly. In there,' he said, jerking his head in the direction of a site office that had been dropped dead centre in a sea of mud.

Inside provided no further clue to why they were there until Raul unrolled a set of architect's plans on the top of a desk.

'The start date was delayed by some planning problems but they tell me they should be finished by the end of summer.'

Nell sat down at the desk and scanned the detailed drawings in front of her.

'I consulted the people from the charity all the way along the line,' Raul said, watching her face. 'And they suggested the adjoining residential facility for respite care.'

'My God, Raul, you've rebuilt the centre!' she gasped, not quite believing what she was seeing.

'Well, not exactly, I thought we'd leave out the wet rot, dry rot and peeling paintwork…'

'You must have been planning this for ages,' she accused.

'A while,' he admitted casually.

'And it must have cost you a small fortune,' she added worriedly.

'It may have escaped your notice, but I am a very rich man.'

'Even so…' Nell felt the hot moisture well in her eyes as she pushed the chair noisily back and got to her feet. She raised her summer-blue tear-drenched eyes to his face and Raul caught his breath.

'You did this for me?'

'I would do anything for you,' he said simply. 'I just thought you might like this…but it's made you cry. I should have bought the necklace. Well, actually…' He hitched the contented baby onto his hip and dug into his trouser pocket with his free hand. 'I got it anyway.' He held out a red velvet box inscribed with the name of a high-class jeweller.

Her hand was shaking when she took it from him and extracted the lovely diamond necklace from within. She held the dazzling bauble to the light. 'It's beautiful.'

'No,' he corrected firmly. 'You are beautiful and you made me the happiest man alive when you married me. When Javier was born I felt as if all the pieces of my life fell into place.'

'That's exactly how I felt too!' she admitted in wonder as she laid her head against her husband's broad chest. She closed her eyes and breathed in the familiar, but exciting—*always exciting*—scent of him. 'Are you going to give me the tour?' she asked when she straightened up.

'Another time. Right now I feel the urge to see you wearing that necklace.'

'I'll need to buy something to wear that will do it justice.'

'I know the perfect thing.'

'My black dress? The one with…' She stopped; Raul was shaking his head.

'Not the black dress, no dress.' His smoky gaze slid down her slender body before returning to her face. 'I want to see the necklace against your smooth skin; nothing else will do it justice.'

An erotic thrill sliced through her body. 'You mean you want to see me…?' She drew a deep breath. 'I think we should go home *immediately*, Raul.'

'You are reading my mind, *querida*.'

'Which is why I'm blushing. You are a very bad man,' she reproached.

The sound of Raul's rich, throaty laugh made her shiver.

'You inspire me to new heights of *badness*,' he admitted.

Nell gave a sultry smile. As goals went this one sounded like something realistic for her to aim towards—to continue to inspire her incredible husband for the rest of their lives together!

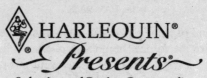

If you enjoyed what you just read,
then we've got an offer you can't resist!

Take 2 bestselling love stories FREE!
Plus get a FREE surprise gift!

Clip this page and mail it to Harlequin Reader Service®

IN U.S.A.
3010 Walden Ave.
P.O. Box 1867
Buffalo, N.Y. 14240-1867

IN CANADA
P.O. Box 609
Fort Erie, Ontario
L2A 5X3

YES! Please send me 2 free Harlequin Presents® novels and my free surprise gift. After receiving them, if I don't wish to receive anymore, I can return the shipping statement marked cancel. If I don't cancel, I will receive 6 brand-new novels every month, before they're available in stores! In the U.S.A., bill me at the bargain price of $3.80 plus 25¢ shipping & handling per book and applicable sales tax, if any*. In Canada, bill me at the bargain price of $4.47 plus 25¢ shipping & handling per book and applicable taxes**. That's the complete price and a savings of at least 10% off the cover prices—what a great deal! I understand that accepting the 2 free books and gift places me under no obligation ever to buy any books. I can always return a shipment and cancel at any time. Even if I never buy another book from Harlequin, the 2 free books and gift are mine to keep forever.

106 HDN DZ7Y
306 HDN DZ7Z

Name	(PLEASE PRINT)	
Address	Apt.#	
City	State/Prov.	Zip/Postal Code

Not valid to current Harlequin Presents® subscribers.

Want to try two free books from another series?
Call 1-800-873-8635 or visit www.morefreebooks.com.

* Terms and prices subject to change without notice. Sales tax applicable in N.Y.
** Canadian residents will be charged applicable provincial taxes and GST.
  All orders subject to approval. Offer limited to one per household.
® are registered trademarks owned and used by the trademark owner or its licensee.

PRES04R   ©2004 Harlequin Enterprises Limited

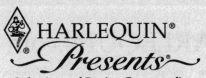

HARLEQUIN®
Presents®

Seduction and Passion Guaranteed!

The O'CONNELLS

by

Sandra Marton

In order to marry, they've got to gamble on love!

Welcome to the world of the wealthy Las Vegas family the O'Connells. Take Keir, Sean, Cullen, Fallon, Megan and Briana into your heart as they begin that most important of life's journeys—a search for deep, passionate, all-enduring love.

Coming in Harlequin Presents®
April 2005 #2458

Briana's story:
THE SICILIAN MARRIAGE
by *Sandra Marton*

Gianni Firelli is used to women trying to get into his bed. So when Briana O'Connell purposely avoids him, she instantly catches his interest. Briana most definitely does not want to be swept off her feet by any man. Or so she thinks, until she meets Gianni....

www.eHarlequin.com   HPTOC